ZOOMED

AN ESSIE COBB SENIOR SLEUTH MYSTERY

Patricia Rockwell

For information, email Cozy Cat Press at:
cozycatpress@gmail.com
or visit our website at:
www.cozycatpress.com

COZY CAT
PRESS

ISBN: 978-1-952579-20-2

Printed in the United States of America

10 9 8 7 6 5 4 3 2 1

Dedicated to all those resilient ladies (and gents) who toughed out the pandemic in true style and showed us all how to be brave.

Chapter 1

Essie Cobb hated the pandemic. And that was saying a lot, because Essie didn't hate much of anything. In fact, as she sat in her recliner with her feet up, she couldn't really think of anything she could honestly say she "hated." Of course, many things were annoying, like the way Victoria Shay almost gargled her iced tea when she drank it, or Eddie Robertson's disgusting habit of squeezing so close to her in the lunch line that she could smell his foul breath, or Melba Brown's obvious cheating at Bingo. But—mused Essie—those were just minor annoyances. She didn't really hate those things—or the people who did them. But the pandemic—now *that* she truly hated it. And with the pandemic going on, she couldn't even see those people or experience their annoying behaviors. Yes, the pandemic was preventing her from living her life at the Happy Haven Assisted Living Facility.

Essie loved Happy Haven; she loved the facility, the staff, and—most of all—the residents, particularly her three best friends Opal, Marjorie, and Fay. *But this stupid pandemic,* reasoned Essie, *is keeping us all apart*. Oh, of course, they could talk on the phone, but it just wasn't the same.

Essie finished up the last square in her crossword puzzle and set the paper aside on her end table where she kept all of her puzzle paraphernalia. *Do these puzzles get easier every day?* she wondered. Each morning, her aide brought her a new puzzle sheet that was provided by management and she quickly completed the crossword, the jumble, and the Sudoku before lunch. *I need more mental stimulation*, she thought. She'd always had that when she and her friends had gathered together and plotted various adventures on a daily basis, but now they all seemed to have lost their energy. Besides, what could they do when they were all stuck alone in their own apartments?

She sipped the last of her cold coffee from the cup on her end table. She glanced at her wristwatch and saw that it was almost lunchtime. *How would I even know it was time to eat anyway?* she thought. As she glanced down at her outfit, she realized that what she was wearing might as well be her bedtime attire. Since the pandemic had started, she couldn't go anywhere outside of her room at the Happy Haven Assisted Living Facility so she didn't need to "doll up" as her late husband John used to say. Before the pandemic, she was careful to dress nicely in a pair of stylish slacks, a colorful shirt or sweater and a polished pair of leather flats. Her hair was always done nicely by Bev at the Happy Haven beauty parlor once a week, and Essie never failed to put on lipstick, and powder her nose. But now? Why bother? The only people she actually interacted with were her two aides—Joey for breakfast and lunch, and Clarice for dinner and bedtime. Her daughter had purchased her some extremely comfortable clothing that was easy to put on so she didn't need any help dressing in the morning any more. Her front-hooking bra was a breeze to slip on; then she just pulled her sweat shirts quickly over her head, and—best of all—her sweat pants were so roomy and stretchy that all she had to do was put both feet in, stand up and—voila—with the addition of sliding into her slippers, she was dressed.

Her aide, Joey, would soon arrive with a lunch tray. Pushing herself out of her armchair, Essie stood slowly and grabbed her nearby trusty red metal rolling walker. Thank goodness for it. It was much better than a cane. She just had to hold on to the top handles and the walkers' little wheels zipped her quickly to wherever she wanted to go. And if she got even slightly winded anywhere along the way, she could take a brief rest by sitting on the comfy seat which was situated right over the vehicle's roomy storage basket.

Essie hobbled down her short hallway to her bathroom so she could clean up. Looking in the mirror, she cringed at the sight of her hair. Before the pandemic, her lovely white shiny locks were always done immaculately in tight little curls all over her head. Now, her hair had grown out and was standing up like unruly tree branches sticking out in all directions. She looked like she'd stuck her finger in an electrical outlet. The beauty shop had been closed during the pandemic and although her night-time aide Clarice helped her wash her hair and shower several times a week, the woman certainly wasn't able to cut her hair or style it or give her a permanent—all routines Essie was used to having done on a regular basis. She simply couldn't think of anything to do to or for her hair to make it even partially presentable. *Maybe it's time to start wearing a bag over my head,* she thought.

Essie returned to her old recliner in her small living room. She scowled when she looked down at the worn out cushion. "All I see there is an impression of my butt," she said to herself. "And it's getting to be a pretty big butt. I need to walk around more. Pathetic pandemic!" She feared she was gaining weight from lack of exercise. She pushed her walker around her living room in an effort to recreate some form of aerobic exercise— huffing and puffing when she was forced to make very sharp turns in the tiny space. As she rounded the room, a flash of red coming between the wooden blinds covering her only window caught her attention. Her room was on the main floor, facing the back of the complex. A row of evergreen trees ran down the back of the facility. Essie pushed her walker over to the window and peered between two of the wooden slats.

A red cardinal was poised on a branch of one of the evergreens. He flitted from the lower branch to a higher branch and then turned straight towards the building and appeared to be looking directly as Essie who was peeking out at him.

"Well, aren't you a handsome fellow," she said to the bird. Cardinals were Essie's favorite birds as anyone could tell by the number of plates, figurines, and pillows featuring the red bird that adorned her living room.

"Good morning to you, sir," she said, as she gave the small creature a tiny salute through the slats of her blinds. The cardinal peered at her hair it seemed to Essie—probably drawn to its extreme shine—then abruptly turned its top-notched head and flew off.

A knock on the door was immediately followed by the door opening and a man entering. He was dressed from top to toe in what looked like a loose-fitting space suit. His head was covered in a yellow plastic helmet and he wore rubber gloves up to his elbows. He carried a tray of food which he immediately placed on Essie's kitchen counter.

"Hi, Joey," said Essie, now out of breath from her recent exercise walk and bird viewing.

"Hey, there, Ms. Essie," replied the young man. "Let's get

your temp checked so you can start on this fancy-lookin' lunch."

"Fancy schmancy," said Essie, as she rolled back to her chair and sat down. Joey came over and stuck a digital thermometer in her mouth, effectively curbing her complaints. "Fanfy my aff! Iff va fame ol bunk!" Joey took her temperature before every meal, since the pandemic had started. They were extremely careful at Happy Haven. A nurse's aide came to see her once a week for a more thorough medical checkup.

The thermometer beeped and Joey removed it, smiling. "You're normal, Ms. Essie."

"Not according to anyone I know," she replied. Joey gave her a smirk.

"Well, from a thermal standpoint anyway."

"I'm really steaming right now, Joey."

"What now? The Sudoku got you stumped?"

"No, Joey. Just flummoxed I guess. This pandemic has really got me down. I miss my friends."

"You can talk to them on the phone."

"It's not the same. I miss seeing them. I miss us all being together. That's when we'd get in a lot of..."

Essie paused abruptly and smiled at Joey. He was new to Happy Haven since the pandemic had started. He didn't know about all the adventures that Essie and her friends had had in the past. Joey placed the tray on her lap. She took her fork and poked at a hard piece of meat in the center of the plate.

"Get in a lot of what, Miss Essie?" asked the figure in the space suit armor.

"Uh, get in...ah...lot of...synchronization. That's it. We'd get synchronized." She smiled sweetly at the young man who was staring down at her through his plastic-covered helmet. "You thought I was going to say 'trouble' didn't you?"

"I don't know what you mean, Miss Essie…"

"You wouldn't. You're too young." She nodded once with authority.

"Oh, I understand synchronicity," said Joey, bending down beside her. "I had a bunch of pals I used to hang with…and we had that 'synchronicity' that I think you're talking about. You know, when one person knows what the other is going to say before the first person says it. We all really understood each other."

"You said 'used' to hang with?"

"Yeah. No time anymore." He started to gather his equipment. "I really need to spend all my time now—you know—working. I live with my parents. I had to move back in. This is the only job I could get and I have to help them out too. They have…a small restaurant…and they're struggling to keep it going during the pandemic…" He looked into Essie's eyes and smiled sadly.

"Oh, Joey, I'm so sorry. I didn't know." She set her tray on the footstool in front of her chair.

"It's okay, Miss Essie. I love working here at Happy Haven. I love the residents. I could do without this uniform though…." He chuckled as he tried to stand and his knee got caught in the folds of his outfit.

"Come here," she ordered. Joey moved around to the side of Essie's chair and she reached up and adjusted the sides of his flowing uniform neatly into the plastic belt at the middle. "There. Now maybe you won't be so likely to trip on this thing."

"I hope so," said Joey. "The last thing I need is to go flying head over heels with a food tray in my hands. Thanks."

"That would be a sight that would make my day," replied Essie, a wicked grin on her face.

Joey headed for the door.

"Wait, Joey," cried Essie, shoving the tray on the footstool towards him. "I can't eat this stuff. I guess they think it's meat. You might as well take the tray back with you now."

Joey came back and stood before her. "Miss Essie, you have to eat."

"No, I don't. It's not like I get any exercise cooped up in here. I bet I've gained twenty pounds just from sitting around all day." She looked down at her waist and pinched the skin around her middle.

"I doubt that. Can't you just take a bite or two?"

"Why? Do you get a bonus if I eat it all?" Joey laughed. "Because if you do, I'll eat it. I'll gag on it, but I'll eat it for you."

"No, I don't get a bonus. I just don't want to see you get sick. You need to keep up your strength. Now is not the time to be daring…"

"Who me? Daring?"

"I've heard stories about you, Miss Essie," the young man whispered, as he bent low and cupped his gloved hand around her ear.

"Well, that's good to know," she said, smiling. "I like being an icon."

"A what?"

"Oh, nothing. Maybe some of those stories about me are true, but how can anyone do anything daring or fun or adventurous when they're stuck in their apartment all day long and can't even go out to visit with their friends?"

"I do understand, Miss Essie." He scowled. Then he bit his lip.

"What's wrong?"

"I'm just thinking. You say you miss your friends. You talk

to them…"

"Yes, but it's not the same as when we all get together in person. I can only talk to one at a time on the phone and even then it's not the same because I can't see them so I can't really know what they're feeling…"

"What about Zoom?" he asked with a smile, arms crossed.

"What's that?" she snorted. "Some wild new sports' car?"

"No, no," he replied. "It's a computer app. You can use it to communicate with a group of people and you can see and hear them all at the same time."

"Hmm, I'm not really into those computers," she said. "My friend Fay is. She used to be a research librarian and she knows all about computers…"

"Does she have a computer?"

"Yes. I have one too, actually. My grandson got it for me years ago. It's on a shelf in my bedroom."

"What about your other friends?"

"Opal and Marjorie? No, I don't think they have any computers."

Joey looked deflated.

"But Fay has several, I know. I don't think she uses them all. In fact, I'm sure she doesn't. Once in her apartment I saw several boxes that had computer names on them."

"Computer names?"

"You know, like Tech this or Mega that. I don't remember. I'll have to ask Fay and that's hard to do because she doesn't talk, but Opal would probably know."

"You know, Miss Essie, if Miss Fay does have a few extra computers—even laptops or iPads or something similar—I could set them up for Miss Opal and Miss Marjorie, and the four of you could Zoom."

"You mean we could see each other…"

"And all talk at the same time," he said, nodding. "Just like you did in the dining room."

"That sounds wonderful, Joey," said Essie. "It wouldn't be the same as actually being together but it would definitely beat out the telephone. Thank you, Joey."

"Miss Essie. I want to see you happy again. And if Zooming with your friends will do that, I'll do anything I can to make it happen."

Joey grudgingly took Essie's tray of uneaten lunch with him, giving her a scolding expression as he left. After he was gone, Essie reached over to her telephone and dialed Opal.

"Opal, it's Essie."

"I know. I recognize your voice," replied a tired sounding woman.

"Do you have a computer?"

"Maybe, somewhere, maybe not, I don't know," Opal said slowly. "Who wants to know?" She yawned.

"I want to know, that's who!" Essie said, peeved. "Don't you think we need to use computers? Get with the times, Opal."

"I have no need for one," said Opal. "The phone is fine with me."

"But is it?" asked Essie. "Is it really fine, Opal? I can't see you when I use the phone…"

"All the better," sighed Opal. "I'm not looking my best these days. I need my hair cut. And the blouse I have on now I would never wear in public."

"Opal, pay attention. If you were looking your best, wouldn't you want us to get together in real life, not just by phone?"

"Oh, I don't know," replied Opal with a deep sigh, "Anything you have to tell me, you can just as easily say over the phone."

"You can't talk to Fay on the phone," said Essie. Their friend

Fay didn't speak, although she could hear and was able to respond in writing and sometimes through gestures. Opal's apartment was next door to Fay's.

"No," said Opal, "but I just write her little notes and stick them under her door and then she sends little notes back to me under my door. We don't tell our aides." Opal cackled.

"That's very daring, Opal," said Essie.

"Oh, yes," replied Opal. "Fay and I are wild and crazy girls." Essie had realized long ago that Opal was the epitome of what was known as the "dead pan."

"Wouldn't it be fun if we could all be together? You and Fay, and me and Marjorie?"

"Essie, I hope you're not planning some shindig, like you used to do…"

"Yes. Like we used to do. We had fun, Opal, when we had those shindigs. Remember? Now, with this pandemic, we all just sit around and mope in our rooms and no one does anything."

"Well, what can we do?" Opal sighed.

"I don't know," said Essie, "but something. And, you know what, Opal, I'm going to start by… Zooming."

"By what?"

"It's a computer thingy. My aide Joey just told me about it. We can all get together and talk and see each other on our computers…"

"Who's we?"

"You and me and Fay and Marjorie…"

"Marjorie doesn't have a computer."

"Well, we'll get her one."

"Where?"

"I don't know; maybe Fay has an extra one."

"Hmm, you know, I think she might. Remember those boxes

she keeps in the corner…"

"Yes, I know. The ones that say 'tech' on them."

"Some of those might be computers."

"Surely they are. Why don't you ask her, Opal? Drop a little note under her door."

"Me? Why should I ask her? It was your idea."

"Please, Opal. You know I can't go out of my apartment and up to Fay's room just to leave her a note without being seen. I'd be in big trouble for leaving my room. You can. Oh, and call Marjorie too. I'm going to try to hook up this old computer of mine that my grandson gave me and figure out the Zoom."

After Essie had convinced a reluctant Opal to write a note to Fay and call their fourth member, Marjorie, the two ladies hung up and went about their appointed duties. Essie wheeled her walker into her bedroom to a tall storage unit where she could see a box on the lower shelf that she knew contained the computer her grandson had given her several years ago. With great care, Essie bent down—her knees creaking in pain the entire time—and pulled the box out of the shelf and placed it onto the seat of her walker. Then she headed back to the living room and pushed her walker over to her sofa where she knew she'd be near an outlet to plug the computer into. Setting the box onto her coffee table, she sat down on the sofa. She took a while to recuperate from this strenuous endeavor. Then, she began to unpack the small laptop computer.

Chapter 2

Within an hour, Essie was done. That is, she had unpacked and examined all of the parts of the computer. She had no idea what part went where, although some items looked decidedly like plugs that would fit into the wall outlet right behind her end table. Just to check, she leaned as far to her left as she could, reaching behind the table to see if her arm was long enough to touch the outlet without having to crawl on the floor. She knew that eventually something would have to go into that hole if this computer was going to work. Now, she just stared at the black device and sighed. *What was Ned thinking of? Why did he ever buy me a computer?* She was too old for something like this. It was way too complicated and far too complex for her to figure out. She was lucky if she could replace a light bulb. *John had always liked to fiddle with gadgets like this*, she thought wistfully, picturing her departed husband. *It's too bad he died before computers came on the scene; he would have loved having one and playing with all of its parts.*

Her phone rang. Annoyed, Essie placed all the computer

parts that were now piled on her lap onto the coffee table, pulled herself up and wheeled herself over to the other end of the sofa where she dropped into her recliner and picked up the receiver.

"Hello."

"Mom?"

"Oh, hello, dear," said Essie, recognizing the voice of her oldest daughter Prudence. "I'm trying to put together that computer Ned sent me."

"What?" said her daughter. "When did he do that?"

"Oh, years ago, when we were working on that....Oh, never mind," said Essie. "What did you want, dear?"

"I'm going shopping. Can I bring you anything?" asked Prudence. "I could drop it off for you at the main desk and someone could bring it up to you. Do you need anything?"

"A technician," mumbled Essie, glancing back at the pile of computer parts sitting on the middle of her coffee table.

"What?"

"No, never mind, dear. You could bring me some of that nice mint liqueur."

"Mom! Alcohol? I meant like do you need any supplies? You know, hand sanitizer? Air sprays? Disinfectant scrubs?"

"Oh, no, dear. The workers here do all of that disinfecting stuff. I don't need to do anything. In truth, I wish I could be responsible for disinfecting something; I might feel more useful."

"Mom, no one expects you to be useful."

"Well, thank you," Essie snorted.

"I didn't mean it that way. I just meant that the best thing you can do right now is stay safe and take care of yourself."

"Right. That's why I asked for the mint liqueur..."

"Oh, Mom, I hope you're not becoming an alcoholic."

"Because I like a little tipple every now and then? Really,

Pru."

"Why don't you let me bring you some nice chocolate mint candies if you want something minty?"

"I don't want something minty…I want something with a kick."

"But you said mint liqueur…"

"I don't care what kind of alcohol it is. Peach liqueur. Vodka. Schnapps. Whiskey. Anything."

"Mom, I am not sneaking alcohol into Happy Haven for you. That's embarrassing."

"For who?"

"For me."

"I thought you wanted to bring me something, and I'm telling you what I want you to bring me and you're telling me you don't want to bring me what I want you to bring me. Oh, never mind. Have Ned call me."

"What?"

"Can you have Ned call me?"

"That's a rather abrupt shift in topic. Just let me get this straight. I am not bringing you any alcohol. But if you want me to bring you something acceptable such as food or magazines or candies, I will be happy to do that. Now, why do you want to talk to Ned? He's not even home now."

"What do you mean he's not home?"

"I mean he's not at his home in Nevada. Claudia said he's on a business trip. He left Shanna and the baby by themselves for the first time since little Henry was born. Claudia's rather worried about them, actually. It's too bad they won't let her go over there during the pandemic but the doctors said Shanna and the baby shouldn't have any visitors now. Claudia's just dying to see that baby. I mean, she and Paul moved all the way out there just to be close to Ned and his new little family. Now that

Ned's out of town, this is the first time Shanna's been all alone with the baby and the baby is still an infant. And with this pandemic going on."

"Oh, she'll be fine."

"How would you know, Mom? Shanna is very shy and…"

"Just because she's shy doesn't mean she can't take care of her own baby. How long will Ned be gone? Did Claudia say? I need to talk to him."

"Why?"

"It's my business."

"You're not planning on involving my nephew in some other harebrained scheme of yours like you did that one time, are you?"

"No. And it wasn't a hare-brained scheme. It was a deviously clever plot."

"He almost died."

"He's fine."

"Now."

"I just want to ask him a computer question."

"Oh. Why?"

"Well, he gave me that old laptop of his several years ago and I just got it out and tried to put it together and—I need some help."

"Oh. How so?"

"I'm not really sure how to plug it in."

"I could see how that could be a problem. Why do you all of a sudden want to use a computer? I thought you thought they were a waste of time."

"I have my reasons. This pandemic has made me realize that I might need to explore options I had once ignored."

"Hmm. I actually like how that sounds, Mom. I'd like to see you doing something constructive rather than just sitting there in your room all day long. When I hear from Claudia, I'll tell her to have Ned call you."

"Thanks, dear."

"I guess that's all I have. If you really don't need me to bring you anything…"

"Nope. I'm fine."

"Okay. Love you. Bye."

"Bye, dear." Essie hung up her phone and hobbled back to the pile of computer parts on the far end of the coffee table. She sat down and picked up the folded paper directions that were included inside the computer box. "Hmmm," she said. "How hard can this be?"

She had managed to attach one strange-looking part to another strange-looking part when the phone rang again.

This time she was greeted with a recorded message from a friendly-sounding woman named Bonnie from the First Neighborhood Bank. As Bonnie typically called several times a day, Essie hung up and started back to the sofa. Happy Haven had offered many seminars on avoiding telephone scams and Essie had attended all of them. She actually considered herself a sort of "phone scam expert." Rule Number One was if the message was recorded, hang up. There were other more complicated rules that she utilized if an actual live person called and tried to sell her something, but the vast majority of calls she received were "Robo-calls" and she just ignored those. When the phone rang immediately after she'd hung up on "Robo-Bonnie," Essie wondered if she'd failed to disconnect from the previous scam call.

"Hello."

"Essie, Opal said we all have to get Zoomed." Essie recognized the voice of her lively red-headed friend Marjorie. "That sounds rather daring, Essie. Does it tickle?"

"No, Marjorie. It's simply a way of conversing with each other over the computer."

"Well, that's ridiculous. We communicate just fine over the telephone." Marjorie's voice sounded light but definite. She didn't like trying new gadgets any more than Essie did, unless they provided sexual stimulation.

"So you wouldn't want to try it with us?"

"Oh, I suppose I would. It's not as if I have anything else to do." Marjorie suddenly sounded sad.

"What's wrong?"

"Oh, nothing that getting out of this apartment of mine and meeting some nice, new gentlemen wouldn't cure. I've been stuck in here so long, that all my parts are getting rusty."

"Marjorie, you're a rascal."

"I have been known to be a rascal, Essie, but it's been so long I'm not sure I'd even remember how to do it anymore."

"Well, while you're trying to remember your rascal moves, you could try Zooming with us."

"I suppose. If I must," said Marjorie with a lilt to her voice. Essie knew that Marjorie loved to flirt and doubted that her interactions with the men at Happy Haven were anything more than that, but with everyone stuck in their own rooms, no one was flirting with anyone these days.

"We just have to find you a computer now," said Essie.

"Oh, I have one," said Marjorie. "Somewhere in my closet. My children got it for me years ago and tried to get me to play games on it but I never could get interested. I guess now that I have nothing better to do, I might as well bring it out of storage and try my hand at...what did you call that again, Essie?"

"Zooming."

"Zooming. Hmmm. There are a few gentlemen here at Happy Haven that I'd like to... *zoom*. If you know what I mean."

"Yes, Marjorie, I'm afraid I do. So you go find that computer of yours—and if you manage to get it to turn on, can you call me back and tell me how you did it?"

"Of course, Essie. Talk to you soon."

The two ladies hung up and Essie wandered back over to her computer parts.

"Oh, no. Now I've forgotten where I was," she moaned. As she'd only managed to attach two parts together, it obviously wasn't very far. It didn't matter, however, as the telephone rang again. Essie scooted back to her phone.

"Hello!"

"Why are you screaming at me, Essie?" said Opal, quietly.

"Oh, hello, Opal. I'm sorry. I was trying to put this computer together. I'm not getting very far. I don't think I'll be able to Zoom. I can't even get this thing assembled."

"Don't worry, Essie. We'll figure it out. Mine is working fine now."

"You got it to work? All by yourself?"

"Well, no, not exactly. My aide helped."

"Your aide?"

"Yes. Joey. He's pretty clever."

"He's my aide too. Maybe he can put this one together for me."

"I'm sure he can," said Opal. "Fay already has hers set up. She has several she uses; she uses computers a lot, but mostly for finding information. She doesn't Zoom."

"How do you know?"

"I've been in her apartment many times, Essie. She has a desk with her main computer set up and two other computers around it; I don't know why she needs so many but she looks at different screens at the same time. But she doesn't Zoom."

"You're sure? With three computers, she must know everything about computing. I bet she knows how to Zoom."

"I don't think so. She doesn't know everything; she mostly just looks at different sites. Did Marjorie talk to you?"

"Yes, she says she has a computer and is going to try to set it up. Do you know if Joey is her aide too?"

"I don't, but I can find out when I see him, and if he isn't, I bet he will still go over to her room and help her. And he can go and make sure Fay is attached to the Zoom too. He's so nice…"

"He is, isn't he? Such a nice young man…" said Essie with a sigh. "We should do something nice for him to thank him for being so kind and helping us all with getting our computers working…"

"That is a lovely idea, Essie. But how? We can't go anywhere?" said Opal with a sigh.

"I know. I'll have my daughter Pru buy him something; she's always pestering me, wanting to bring me things. I'll tell her what we're doing and why we want a gift for Joey…"

"Essie, you know, just getting him a gift is…I don't know, not really enough. He's going through a lot and his family is …"

"Yes, I know," replied Essie. "They lost their restaurant…or are about to lose it. Joey had to move back in with his parents to save money. I don't think this job at Happy Haven is his dream job—taking care of a lot of old ladies—and a few gentlemen."

"Don't ever forget those gentlemen, Essie. You know we outnumber them eight to one," Opal reminded her. One of Happy Haven's selling jingles was, "Where the women outnumber the men eight to one."

"How can I forget? No one will let me forget," said Essie. "But, we really should help Joey; he's such a nice boy. Let me ask my daughter. I'm sure she can come up with something."

"Okay, Essie. I'm going back to trying to figure out my computer."

"Me too. I'm sure you'll figure yours out before I figure out mine."

"I doubt it. Bye."

"Bye." No sooner had Essie hung up the phone, and waddled back to her computer project, than the phone rang again.

"I am so popular today," she cried out loud as she stomped back to her phone and plopped back down in her recliner again. "Yes?"

"Hi, Grandma. It's Ned. I hear you have a computer problem."

Chapter 3

Ned was not only Essie's oldest grandchild, he was her oft-time compatriot in crime. They had, on several occasions, plotted together some projects that none of Essie's children had approved of. Of course, that never mattered to Essie. She always considered Ned her first—and best—grandchild. The fact that he was some sort of technical genius had been helpful in some of their past adventures, but now she needed his assistance for something more mundane.

"Oh, Ned. I need to Zoom and I can't figure out how to put this computer you gave me together."

"Zoom? Grandma, sounds like you're joining the 'woke' crowd."

"Oh, I'm awake all right, but I'd like to just Zoom with Opal and Marjorie and Fay so we can see each other when we talk and so we can all talk together at the same time, but I can't get the pieces of the computer you gave me to fit together."

"That'll never do," said Ned, "Tell me what pieces you have."

"Okay," Essie replied. "There's this big black device that folds up and opens. There's this long cord with a box in the middle and a plug at the end. There's a smaller box with a doohickey on it."

Ned proceeded to guide Essie through the process of setting up her laptop computer, from plugging it into her wall outlet, to turning it on, signing on, and arranging her screen settings. He explained to her how to turn it off and on. He showed her where the camera was located and where the microphone was and how to adjust both.

"You'll need to know that for Zooming, Grandma." Ned told her about the camera and mic settings. "You might want to play with your mic and your camera so you can see how you look and sound on your screen before you actually start Zooming. "Let's try it now." He walked her through the procedure. Essie pressed all the rights buttons and soon she was astounded when she saw her own face in a small box on the screen.

"Oh my, it's me," she said, delighted.

"Good," said Ned. "Do you look as pretty as you are?"

"I look like me," she said, "and that's hardly pretty, Ned, you charmer."

He chuckled. "Let's make sure you have volume." He directed her to press various dials and buttons and soon Essie had recorded her own voice and played it back.

"Is that what I sound like?"

"Just like you."

"Oh my, I sound like a big gargly old frog," she said.

He chuckled some more and showed her how to set up the Zoom app.

"Okay, Grandma, you're all set up. Do you want to try a Zoom practice session?"

"How do I do that?"

"See that blue box at the top left? You can set your time and day there and invite people by their email addresses. I'm going to set up a Zoom chat now at my end and invite you. When you get the invite, accept it and we will be officially Zooming. Can you do that?"

"I think so," said Essie, hovering her finger over the laptop's touchpad. Suddenly, the screen changed and a sign popped up asking Essie if she wanted to Zoom with Ned Presser. She clicked 'yes' and, suddenly, live images of both her and Ned appeared on the screen.

"Oh, my," she said. "Ned, this is wonderful."

"That can't be you, Grandma," replied Ned. "That looks like some hot young swinger. Do you see me? Do you see both of us?"

"Yes, I see both of us. This is amazing. Oh, Ned, it's almost as if we are together in the same room. I can hear you and see you as if you were really here with me."

"That's the idea, Grandma. That's what Zoom is all about."

They talked and laughed and played with various buttons and tried different special effects that Zoom would allow until Essie was feeling fairly comfortable with her new skill.

"Okay, Grandma, I think you're a Zoom expert now. Let's make you a Zoom ID and get you scheduled for your first Zoom meeting with your pals. I'll check to be sure you have link invites to send to your three friends. When should we set it up for?"

"Oh, my, let me think," she responded. "I don't know how long it will take them all to get their computers working and get this Zoom app thing set up like this..."

"Do you want me to help them?"

"No," she said, "at least not now. Let me check and see how they're doing. I know Fay won't need any help. My aide Joey has been helping Opal set up her computer. He might be able to help with the Zoom part too. If I need you, Ned, I'll let you know. You've done enough. I know you need to get back to work…"

"I'm never too busy to help my favorite grandmother…"

"Thank you, and lots of love to Shanna and the baby."

"Thanks, Grandma. She's a little lonely with me being away for work for so long what with this pandemic going on. But I'll be back home next week. It's been a nice break being able to help you. Otherwise, I'm just stuck in a hotel."

"Are you staying safe, Ned?"

"Oh, yes, safe—and bored," he responded. "We computer nerds do so much of our work online anyway that I hardly ever need to put on my mask. I truly don't even see why I have to be out of town except my boss wanted me to go to this darn convention."

"Well, keep safe. I don't want anything bad to happen to you."

"And I don't want anything bad to happen to you, Grandma. Lots of hugs from me and Shanna and the baby."

"Hugs back." Essie said. They hung up and Essie looked around at her computer, now nicely set up on her coffee table. She could still see herself in the little square as she hadn't clicked out of the Zoom program, even though Ned had left and the square with his image had disappeared. Essie took the time to stare at herself on the screen. She moved her face around, tipping her head up and then down, opening her eyes more, then closing them. She turned her face right, then left, trying to see which presentation was the most attractive in the little box.

"Oh, this is stupid," she said eventually, "and incredibly vain." She clicked the "off" button and closed the computer lid. She unplugged the device from her wall. However, she left the computer and all of its parts still sitting on her coffee table. She planned for it to get a lot of use in the forthcoming days.

Chapter 4

The next day, Essie awoke feeling a certain degree more hopeful than she had in the last six months. She quickly slipped on her pandemic outfit of sweatshirt, sweatpants, and slippers and she was ready to go. Now she had a project that she was looking forward to. She reminisced fondly about some of her previous adventures that had brought her so much happiness. She remembered that at the time, many of those adventures had seemed scary, impossible, and even downright dangerous. She didn't think that Zooming with her friends on a computer would prove to be even slightly dangerous, but it did hold the potential to be a learning exercise. She would discover something new about technology; and they all would get to know each other better. It sounded wonderful, and Essie was excited to get started.

As she whipped out to her living room, she felt a new burst of energy. It was probably the way most people felt whenever they embarked on a new project. She pushed her walker over to her living room window and peeked between the slats to see if her friendly cardinal was anywhere around. She stood there for quite some time staring out at the field and trees behind Happy Haven. There was a slight breeze. She was enjoying the view; it was all so peaceful. All of a sudden, the red bird appeared out of nowhere and landed on a low branch of the evergreen in front of Essie's window. He was so close, that Essie could have almost touched him if it weren't for the window pane. He looked straight at her. "Hey, there, fellow," she said softly. "No pandemic for you, right? You can come and go wherever and whenever you like." The bird tipped its head to the side as if to say, "So true," then it flew off and was gone. Essie remained at her window a few minutes more then headed back to her bathroom to get ready..

By the time Joey arrived with her breakfast, Essie had already fixed her hair and make-up. She wanted to look good for the Zoom meeting later and she knew her friends would be able to see her on their computers. *A little vanity isn't a bad thing*, she reasoned.

"Miss Essie, you look like you're ready for a party," said Joey as he entered with her breakfast tray. Essie met him at the kitchen counter.

"My friends and I are going to Zoom today, Joey," she said, opening her mouth for her temperature check as Joey set down her tray. He pulled the thermometer from his side bag and stuck it in Essie's mouth.

"Wonderful, Miss Essie," he said. "I helped your friend Miss Opal. She seems ready to go for your meeting too. I showed her the settings for Zoom and how to use the mic and camera. She caught on really fast. Miss Opal is a smart cookie."

"Mimifrafif Uffifpam"

"What?" said Joey, then quickly removed the thermometer as it beeped.

"I said Opal was an administrative assistant for some big executive before she retired," said Essie. "I don't know if she knows how to Zoom but she could surely type fast and do things like that…"

"Oh, she can Zoom," said Joey, putting away his equipment and leading Essie into her living room where she settled in her recliner. He placed her breakfast tray on her lap.

"Pancakes," cried Essie. "Blueberry pancakes. They haven't had this for ages. Maybe that chef has gotten his act together down there in the kitchen . . ."

"I don't know about that," said Joey, "because I don't really know the kitchen staff, but one of the other aides said the main chef was out with Covid and they had to get a new chef."

"Oh, no," cried Essie. "Is he okay?"

"Nobody knows," replied Joey, "but he must be pretty sick for them to replace him permanently."

"Yes, he must be," said Essie. "Oh my. I had no idea. I remember him. He would sometimes walk around the dining room and ask us if we enjoyed our meals. I mean, what could we say? If we said we didn't enjoy our meal, what would he do? It's not as if we could choose to go to a different place to eat, but he seemed like a jovial fellow and nice and …." She bent her head and took a deep breath.

"I'm sorry, Miss Essie. I didn't mean to upset you. Actually, it's remarkable that he's the only staff member that I've heard of who has actually caught the virus. And I don't think he caught it here. They're really super cautious at Happy Haven with disinfecting and safety. Well, I mean, look at me. I look like a space invader."

They laughed.

"I'm being so self-centered, Joey. I've only been worried about how I feel. And all I feel is really lonely and bored. And here our chef has the virus, you have to work at a place where you don't want to work, your parents are struggling to keep their business…. Oh, it's all so sad."

"I know, Miss Essie. But, truth be told, meeting you and the other residents here has actually helped me maintain my spirit during all this time. Everyone here is so positive and kind. I used to work in a corporate setting and it was soul crushing. I like the personal relationships I've developed here, and I wouldn't change it for anything."

"I bet you'd change it for a reasonable salary," she said.

"Well, that's the only problem," he replied, "but everything else is great. Now, why don't you show me your computer and how you go Zooming."

"I assume you know how to Zoom, Joey," Essie said, opening her laptop.

"I do," he said, "I Zoom with some of my friends who have moved away and have jobs now out on the West coast. We Zoom every weekend."

"You can check me out, and then, I was wondering…" she hesitated, "if maybe you could go over to my friend Marjorie's room and help her set up her computer and teach her how to Zoom too so she'll be ready for our meeting today?"

"I would be honored to help you and your ladies in any way I can," he said, glancing over at the tray in front of her. The pancakes had disappeared. "Now where did those go?"

"I slurped them down," she said. "They were fabulous."

"It makes my heart feel good to see you eat with such gusto, Miss Essie."

The two of them spent the next few minutes looking over Essie's computer setup. Joey had Essie show him how she could turn the computer on and open her Zoom app.

When he was satisfied she would be ready for her meeting

later that day, he picked up her tray and headed to the door. "Oh, what room is your friend in?"

"Marjorie is in 226. I'll call and tell her to expect you."

"Great. I just have to deliver a few more trays and then I'll get right over to see her."

"Thank you, Joey. You're the best."

"No, you're the best, Miss Essie." And he was off, whistling.

Chapter 5

Later that day, Essie was getting very excited for the first Zoom meeting. She had phoned Marjorie and Opal and they had decided to hold their meeting at three o'clock. Essie had followed Ned's directions and had created a Zoom invitation and sent it to all three of her friends. As Fay didn't really speak, Essie hoped that Opal would put a note under Fay's door so she would know about the meeting and join them, because Essie couldn't phone her. She realized how much she missed Fay and was really looking forward to seeing her even if Fay would probably not say a word. She had no doubt that Fay would understand how the Zoom worked and would be able to make it work on her own computer. Now all Essie had to do was wait until the appointed time.

She kept going back and forth to her restroom to comb her hair and powder her nose. She realized it was foolish behavior. In the past, she had never bothered with refreshing her make-up when she met her gal pals in the dining room, but for some reason, today's meeting seemed so special. She was also worried about whether she would be able to handle all the bells and buttons that Ned had trained her to use. There was a lot to remember.

But finally, the magic hour arrived. Essie sat on her sofa. Her computer was plugged in, turned on, and her Zoom screen was brought up. At exactly three o'clock, Essie pressed the button to open the Zoom meeting and her image appeared in the "host" box at the top left-hand corner. She smiled for the camera.

"Hello, everyone. It's Essie. Where are you all?"

She didn't have long to wait. In a few seconds, the others started to arrive. Opal's square popped up first."

"Hello, Essie," said her friend. "You look just like....well, just like Essie."

"Thank you, Opal. I can see it's you and that you have on your namesake opal necklace if I needed any clue to remind me of your identity."

Opal smiled and fingered her necklace. Opal's long neck was enhanced by the fact that she wore her long hair on top of her head in a neat bun.

A third screen popped open. Essie immediately recognized their silent buddy Fay. Fay was sitting in her wheelchair, looking cheerful and happy as she typically did. She smiled and waved shyly, her little fringe of brownish-grey bangs hanging a bit lower than the last time Essie had seen her. She pointed a finger up and to the corner of the screen.

"Oh, Fay, you're here. Wonderful. What is it, Fay? What are you pointing to?" asked Essie.

"She's pointing at something," said Opal.

"I see that, Opal," replied Essie, "but what is she pointing to?"

"I think she must mean something on the Zoom screen. Let me see...."

Essie could see Opal's head tip sideways as she was obviously searching the computer for Fay's clue. Fay continued to smile and point.

Essie looked at the various headings along the right edge of the screen. She noticed one button that said "Chat."

"Opal, there's a button here that says 'Chat.' Do you think she's pointing to that?"

"I don't know," said Opal. "Let me see. Oh, yes. That's it, Essie. Press the button. Fay is talking to us."

Essie pressed the "Chat" button and, sure enough, she spotted Fay's name listed on the screen along with her comments. Fay was greeting them, telling them how much she missed them and telling them she would add her thoughts via this "Chat" button.

"Wonderful, Fay," said Essie. "I have missed you so much." Fay smiled broadly and nodded her head up and down and pointed her hands from her own heart straight through the screen at Essie.

"Hey, hey," said a new voice. A fourth box popped open and they could all see the latest addition to their meeting—Marjorie, who was looking especially perky.

"Marjorie, you made it," said Essie. "Did Joey help you set up your Zoom screen?"

"He did," replied the redhead in the fourth screen. "Essie Cobb, you never told me your aide was such a hunk. I'm going to complain to management. My aide is that frowsy old dolt Bertha Grimes."

"He's my aide too, Marjorie," chimed in Opal, a hint of superiority in her voice.

"As if you'd know what to do with a young man like that, Opal." Marjorie giggled and merrily shook her locks of bright red curls.

"Just like old home week," said Essie as she glanced around her screen. It wasn't exactly like being in the Happy Haven dining room, but it ran a close second. Her pals were all together again—and they were slinging those zingers already.

"Essie," said Marjorie, "what have you done to your hair?"

"Nothing, Marjorie," replied Essie, "that's the problem. It's growing out and I can't get to Bev to fix it in nice curls."

"You mean those tight little knots all over your head," said Opal, patting her own neat little grey bun.

"I'm famous for my tight little curls," said Essie, brushing her hand over her hair in embarrassment.

"Your curls look nice, Marjorie," said Opal, "how do you keep them so smooth without Bev?"

"Oh, I do my own," replied Marjorie, patting her hair. "I do my own dye jobs and I curl it myself and style it myself. I surely wouldn't trust that aide of mine Bertha."

"I'm so glad I don't have to worry about mine growing out," said Opal. "I just roll it up into a bun. Oh, but, girls, look at Fay's hair. She's been cutting it herself."

"I didn't want to say anything," said Marjorie, scowling. "Fay, you really got carried away with those scissors, didn't you?"

To this, Fay just fluffed her bangs with her hands and tossed her short hair around and then typed furiously.

"What's she saying?" said Marjorie.

"Here," said Opal, "just read the 'Chat.' She says she cuts her bangs short enough to keep her hair out of her eyes."

"That's the spirit, Fay," said Essie. "You're a utilitarian. You believe in 'Do it yourself.' I wouldn't want to impose on my evening aide to help me with hairdos. She has enough to do just helping me bathe and wash my hair."

"Essie," said Marjorie, "I'll send you some of my foam

curlers and a bonnet. You can put them in yourself when you wash your hair and sleep in them overnight and in the morning, your hair will be curly and you won't look so much like a— well—ogre."

"You don't have to…"

"It would be my pleasure," said Marjorie, "I have so many hair supplies I don't know what to do with them all."

"Well, thank you, Marjorie," said Essie. "I'll give it a try."

"So," said Marjorie after a pause, "how is everyone doing? I hear so far that no residents at Happy Haven have come down with the virus, which is great."

"I heard that our chef has it," added Essie.

"I heard that too, poor man," said Opal.

"Do any of you have any other medical problems?" asked Marjorie. "What about regular coughs or colds or other weird symptoms?"

"Nothing like that," said Opal, "but I do have one very strange symptom. It's sort of a thrumming in my knee…"

"Do you mean like a musical sound?" asked Essie.

"I don't know if you can hear it," replied Opal, "but I feel as though there's a sound that goes along with it. It feels as if my knee is sort of buzzing."

"Maybe you've got the bee's knees," laughed Marjorie.

"Is it painful?" asked Essie.

"Not really," said Opal.

Fay waved her arms and then pointed to the upper corner of the screen. They all looked up and followed her finger to the "Chat" button. When Essie pressed the button, she saw that Fay had contributed a suggestion for Opal. She asked Opal if she'd had any orthopedic replacement surgery and said that if so, maybe she was sensing a ringing from the implant.

"Great idea, Fay," said Essie.

"I did have orthopedic surgery once," said Opal, frowning, "I can't remember when, but…"

"What was replaced?" asked Marjorie.

"My left hip," said Opal.

"But you said your knee was buzzing," said Essie.

"That's true," said Opal. "Do you think they might be connected in some strange alien way?"

"Does it hurt, Opal?" asked Essie.

"Not really; it's just strange," replied Opal.

At that moment, a fifth window opened up and a new image appeared in a new box. It was an elderly lady with straw-colored hair worn all fluffed up and curled gently around her face. The woman appeared to be able to see the other women in the meeting.

"You're not Will," she said, her eyes appearing to dart from Essie to Opal to Fay to Marjorie. "Where's Will? Who are you?"

"Hello," said Essie, obviously confused. "I'm Essie. Who are you?"

"I'm Carolyn," said the newcomer. "Where's Will?"

"I don't know," replied Essie. "We were just having a friendly Zoom meeting."

"I need to see Will. Where is he? They said he would be here."

"Marjorie, Opal, do you know who this lady is?" Essie asked.

"I've never seen her," said Opal.

"Me neither," replied Marjorie.

By now, Fay was gesturing and pointing to the "Chat" button. Essie quickly pressed the button where Fay had written, "Maybe she wrote the wrong Zoom address into her browser. Ask her what address she wrote in?"

"Good job, Fay," said Essie.

"Will, where are you? Who are you people?" said the new blond lady again, now becoming obviously distressed.

"Um, Carolyn?" said Essie, "Can you tell me what address you typed into your Zoom?"

"What?" said the lady. "What? I don't know what you mean. They said I could see Will here. They said Will would be here. Will is gone. They said I could find Will here on this computer and I could see him. I need Will. Please."

"Essie," said Opal, "she's confused. This isn't helping. Let me talk to her. Hello, Carolyn. My name is Opal. We want to help you find Will."

"No, you don't. Will! Where are you?" The lady in the small square window on the screen looked around hysterically and suddenly her face disappeared.

"No, Carolyn!" cried Essie, "Don't go away. We want to help you. Now see what you've done, Opal."

"What I've done?"

"It was your idea to tell her we'd help her," said Essie.

Oh, dear," said Opal. "Now what do we do?"

"What can we do?" asked Marjorie, "Fay had the best idea— to find the address she used to enter this Zoom meeting. Maybe we could use that to track her down."

Fay was waving her arms again. They all opened the "Chat" button. Fay had posted that she would try to track down the woman from her ID link which had popped up when she entered the chat.

"Oh, Fay, that would be the thistle's whistle," said Essie, "I feel that we didn't help her at all and she really seemed like she needed our help. Maybe we should do this Zoom again and see if we can find this Carolyn and see what we can do to help her find her Will. What do you all think?"

"Why don't we Zoom again tomorrow at the same time and maybe by then, Fay will have located Carolyn," said Opal.

"That sounds great, Opal," said Marjorie. "And if any of us can think of any other way to help Carolyn or track her down, we can discuss how to do it tomorrow. Is that okay with you, Fay?"

They all looked at Fay's image in her square where Fay was nodding and smiling. Then she paused and gave them all a "thumbs up."

Chapter 6

Essie couldn't sleep that night. She tossed and turned. The image of the distraught Carolyn kept popping into her mind and she couldn't help but muse over and over who she might be and who Will might be and how she could help them. In the morning, she was up like a flash even though she hadn't gotten much sleep. She was anxious to get busy on her plan to find Carolyn.

"This is a real mystery, Essie Cobb," she said aloud to herself, "and mysteries are something you are very good at solving." As she entered her living room, she checked out her window briefly but didn't see the cardinal anywhere in the tree. "I can't wait around today for you, Red," she said and then smiled, liking the name she'd picked for him.

When Joey arrived with her breakfast, she was dressed in her pandemic uniform of sweatshirt and pants and ready to go. She even opened the door for him and followed him into her kitchen. They did their medical duties first.

"Miss Essie, you seem full of energy this morning. Did you

do that Zoom meeting with your friends yesterday?"

"We did, Joey," she said. "It turned out quite well. I want to thank you for all your help in getting us all set up and training us too."

"It was my pleasure, Miss Essie. Did all of the ladies participate?"

"Oh, yes. All four of us. And there was a fifth lady too." By now, Essie was seated and eating scrambled eggs and bacon.

"Who was that?" asked Joey. He knew that Essie knew many of the women at Happy Haven and it would not have been a surprise for Essie's Zoom group to have grown to include a much larger number of participants.

"Carolyn," said Essie, waiting to see if Joey might recognize the name.

"Carolyn who?" he asked.

"That's what I'd like to know," said Essie. "She just showed up on the screen while the four of us were talking and sort of took over…"

"Wow," said Joey, "sort of a Zoom wedding crasher, but without the wedding."

"Right," said Essie. "Do you know any Carolyns here at Happy Haven?"

"I don't take care of any, but that doesn't mean anything. There are lots of residents and lots of aides. I couldn't begin to know all of the names of all the residents."

"Could you find out if we have any Carolyns here, Joey?"

"Sure. I'll check the roster when I go back downstairs. You look like you've finished off your breakfast."

"I have, but I'd like to keep my coffee cup if you don't mind. I need energy today and I need my wits about me."

"Oh, Miss Essie, I think you always have your wits about you. Can I do anything for you before I leave?"

"No, thank you, Joey. Just check to see if we have any Carolyns and let me know what you find out."

"I will, Miss Essie. See you at lunch time."

He headed out with his plastic uniform skirt flying in his wake, and Essie took the new puzzle sheet he'd brought with breakfast and whipped through it. *These puzzles,* she mused, *were ridiculously easy. What they ought to do is give you a sheet of paper that asks you to track down a woman whose name is Carolyn and that's all you know about her.*

Before she could think about what to do next, the phone rang.

"Hi, Mom. Did I get you out of bed?" Essie recognized the sprightly voice of her youngest daughter Claudia.

"Of course not. I'm up and busy. I already finished all the puzzles."

"I hear you and Ned are in cahoots again. What dirty deed do you have him involved in this time?"

"Nothing dirty, Claudia. He helped me set up that old computer he gave me and then he showed me how to do a Zoom meeting."

"Wow, Mom. That's pretty fancy. I've never done Zoom. I hear it's complicated."

"It is rather sophisticated, dear, but Ned showed me how to do it and we had our first Zoom meeting yesterday afternoon."

"Who did you Zoom with?"

"Oh, you know, my friends Opal and Marjorie and Fay....and some strange woman I'd never met before named Carolyn."

"Why did you invite a stranger to your Zoom meeting?" asked Claudia.

"I didn't invite her; she just showed up."

"Oh my. That wasn't very polite. What did you tell her?"

"Well, actually, she was pretty upset. She was looking for someone named Will and I think she got into our Zoom meeting by accident…"

"How could she do that?"

"I have no idea. Ned never told me something like that could happen. The next time you talk to him, ask him what I should do when someone barges in like that?"

"I will. That was really quite thoughtless on this Carolyn woman's part…"

"Actually," said Essie, "I felt sorry for her. She seemed lost. As I said, she was looking for someone named Will and she thought he was in our meeting and even though we told her he wasn't, and that we didn't know who he was, she kept insisting he was there and asked why we were keeping him from her. She was very upset. All of us are concerned about her and we're going to work on trying to find out who she is and see if we can help her find this Will she's looking for.."

"Well, I hope you succeed, and if I talk to Ned, I'll definitely tell him about your rather strange first Zoom meeting."

"Thank you, dear. How are you doing?"

"Oh, I'm fine. I spend a lot of time talking to Shanna on the phone; she's so worried with the new baby and Ned gone so much now. I wish I could be there for her, but this stupid pandemic forces me to stay home with Paul. We're bored together. Here I have a new grandchild—my first one—and I can't even play with him. But the last thing I want to do is risk giving some virus to Shanna or the baby. But believe me, Mom, I would so much rather be there with her and helping her than loafing around my house. My kids are all grown and my husband doesn't need me. I have the time to be a good grandma now but…"

"I know, dear——the stupid pandemic. Anyway, you can talk

to Shanna and keep her spirits up over the phone. Call me if you need your own spirits boosted."

"I will, and be careful with that Zooming. Who knows who may drop in on your next session? Then again, maybe it'll be a movie star."

They laughed and then hung up.

Essie sipped her coffee as she contemplated her next move. As she drank, the phone rang again.

"Essie, it's Opal. I'm calling to report what Fay found out— or rather didn't find out. She tried to trace Carolyn by the link that she used to join our Zoom meeting and Fay said it led to a senior center in Bancroft Falls, New York."

"Oh, Opal, that's sound promising."

"Not so fast," replied Opal. "I called Bancroft Falls information and got the phone number and I just got though with calling them. It's not an assisted living facility like Happy Haven. It's sort of an open center where any senior with a Medicare card can come in and get various services—like counseling, legal aid, etc. It's called Bancroft Falls Senior Citizens' Services Center. I talked to a clerk there. They have a computer room and seniors can come in and use their computers whenever they like. I asked him if a Carolyn had used one of their computers yesterday and he said he wasn't allowed to give out that information."

"That's just the shoes' booze," said Essie. "Now how will we ever find her?"

"We know she lives in Bancroft Falls, New York," said Opal.

"And how many Carolyns do you suppose live there?"

"Well, maybe not many," suggested Opal. "It's probably a small town."

"Opal, it has a senior center," declared Essie. "What small town has such a thing?"

"One that is thoughtful and compassionate and cares about its elderly residents," replied Opal in a soothing voice.

"Opal, you are such a goody two shoes."

"Really, Essie, have you ever heard of Bancroft Falls, New York?"

"No, but there are plenty of large towns I've never heard of."

"Just wait a minute. I think we're getting ahead of ourselves here."

"What are we going to do? Put out an ad asking all the Carolyns in Bancroft Falls, New York, to call us?"

"No, of course not. Maybe she'll call us again," said Opal.

"Why would she? You said she called from a computer room in a senior center in Bancroft Falls. How likely is it that she'll return there and somehow accidentally get her computer hooked to our Zoom meeting here again?"

"Not likely. We could put an ad in the Bancroft Falls newspaper—if they have one."

"What if she doesn't read the newspaper?" asked Essie.

"I guess it's a lost cause, Essie. We're never going to be able to contact this woman."

"But...but...she can't find Will, and she needs to find him," said Essie.

"I know."

"Do you think Will is her husband?" Essie asked, feeling forlorn.

"Or maybe her son?" offered Opal.

"We do know some things, Opal. If Carolyn went to this senior center to use the computer, we know she's mobile and can get around. She probably doesn't have Covid."

"Yes, I think we can assume that."

"What if Will became ill while she was out and managed to get to a hospital and then fell unconscious and has no way to tell the staff who he is or how to contact Carolyn..."

"Could be," agreed Opal. "Or she visits the senior center regularly and was just calling a friend named Will whom she hadn't seen for some time..."

"She seemed awfully upset for Will to be just a friend," said Essie.

"It's a mystery, Essie."

"I'm not giving up," said Essie.

"I figured as much," said Opal. "We can discuss it more this afternoon on our Zoom call."

The two ladies hung up.

And almost instantaneously the phone rang again.

"Yes?" said Essie, grateful that she hadn't trudged all the way over to her computer before having to turn around and come right back.

"Grandma," said a voice she knew was Ned's. "I hear from Mom that you had quite a surprising first Zoom meeting."

"Oh, Ned," said Essie, "It's a mystery. This strange woman named Carolyn just popped up on the screen and started demanding that we show her someone named Will. It was as if she thought we were hiding this Will from her. She was so upset. Then she just left and we couldn't find out anything from her, so we don't really know what to do now—or if there's anything we can do now."

"That is strange, Grandma. I've been in many a Zoom meeting and never had anyone crash in like that. Sounds like you just attract excitement—even on the computer."

"My friend Fay was able to track her Zoom ID."

"Great."

"Not really. Seems it was connected to a senior center in Bancroft Falls, New York, and Opal called it but they can't—or won't—give out anyone's name."

"So you don't know anything about this Carolyn except that she's from Bancroft Falls, New York, and is looking for someone named Will."

"Right. Not much to go on, is it, fellow detective?" asked Essie.

"Nope," agreed Ned. "But let's not give up just yet. There are other avenues we can try. When do you gals do your next Zoom meeting?"

"This afternoon at three o'clock."

"Would you mind if I dropped by?" he asked.

"Of course not, Ned. We would be honored to have you attend."

"Well, then, I'll be there. Can you send me an invite? You remember how to do that? You know my address like I showed you?"

"I do. I remember, Ned. I think it will be very helpful to have you join us."

"Okay, Grandma. See you then. I'd better get some work done, or my boss is going to fire me for spending all my time with you."

"Oh, Ned, no. We don't want to …."

"I'm kidding, Grandma," he said. "I'll see you at three."

Shortly after Essie concluded her conversation with Ned, Joey arrived with her lunch. Essie was surprised because she couldn't believe it was already lunchtime.

"Oh, Joey," she said. "I thought you just brought my breakfast."

"Nope," he replied. "The morning just whizzed by. But, I did manage to check the resident roster to see if we have any Carolyns—and we don't. We have two Carols and a Carol Lee, but no Carolyn." He set her grilled cheese sandwich and tomato soup on her hassock.

"Oh, sorry, Joey," she replied. "I should have contacted you. Opal found out that the woman who barged into our Zoom meeting yesterday is from Bancroft Falls, New York."

"New York?" asked Joey.

"Yes," said Essie, digging into her soup. "She was calling from a senior center there."

"That sounds good. Could you find out who she is?"

"No. They won't give out the name of anyone who uses their facilities. It's not an assisted living home like Happy Haven. It's just a place where any senior on Medicare can go and use the facilities. I guess this Carolyn went there to use the computer to try to find this Will. Maybe someone there knows who she is, but nobody will say."

"Hmm," said Joey. "That is a problem, but it doesn't sound insurmountable."

"It doesn't? How so?" asked Essie, melted cheese dripping down her chin.

"It seems that what you need is a good cover story," he suggested.

"Oh," said Essie, nodding. "Of course. You mean lie. I'm not averse to lying if it's for the greater good, but the question is what lie should I tell?"

"I don't know, Miss Essie," Joey replied, "but I'm guessing you ladies will figure out the perfect concoction to get the information you need from this place."

"Joey," said Essie, "you have heard tales about me, haven't you?"

The two smiled at each other and eyebrows were raised. Then they went about their afternoons—Joey to work and Essie to finish the sandwich she'd saved in a paper napkin and contemplate how to extract the information about the unknown Carolyn from the senior center in Bancroft Falls.

Chapter 7

No sooner had Joey stepped out the door, than Essie downed the rest of her sandwich and picked up a small note pad and a pencil and dialed the Happy Haven front desk and asked for an outside operator.

"I want to call Bancroft Falls, New York," she said to the friendly voice when the operator came on the line. She heard some clicks and then another voice.

"What number, please?" said the operator in Bancroft Falls, New York.

"I don't know the number but it's the Bancroft Falls Senior Citizens' Service Center," replied Essie.

She waited while the operator pressed buttons and sounds rang through her receiver. Soon there was a ring tone and the phone was answered. "Bancroft Falls Senior Citizens' Service Center," said a friendly voice.

"Oh, hello. I'm not sure you can help me."

"I'll certainly try, ma'am," said the nice-sounding lady at the other end. "What can I do for you?"

"Um, my...uh sister was in there yesterday afternoon, I believe, using your computers. Um, she seems to be, uh, missing and we're trying to track her down. Apparently, your facility was the last place where we know for sure she was. I just thought that if you had a record of her being there...and maybe what she was looking for, it would help us locate her?" Essie knew this bogus story would probably never fool any clerk in any government facility, but she had to give it a try.

"Oh, I'm so sorry," said the lady. "What is your sister's name?"

"Carolyn," said Essie, proud that she could provide the clerk with some actual true information.

"And her last name?"

"Well, that I'm not so sure of."

"You don't know your sister's last name?" said the now suspicious clerk.

"Well, yes, it's Franklin." Essie gave the clerk her own maiden name. *Boy,* she thought, *that's thinking, Essie. Obviously it wouldn't be Cobb as that was John's name and if she's my sister she would have my maiden name—that is, if she isn't married. But what if she is married?* Then it dawned on her that her sister would probably be married and have a totally different name and it wouldn't be the name that this Carolyn had anyway because Essie was making all of this up.

"Franklin," said the clerk, seemingly looking for something. "Carolyn Franklin. I'm looking at the sign-in sheet from yesterday's users and I don't see any Carolyn Franklin here..."

"Or maybe just a Carolyn? I fear she's trying to hide from her, uh, her abusive husband, so she may not have given her correct last name." *That's right, Essie. Just make it as convoluted as possible.*

"Oh, wait. There is a Carolyn. But this is a Carolyn Harper.

Do you think she made up that name?" Essie jotted down the last name on her little pad of paper. So much for all that privacy hoo-ha that the man at the center had given Opal yesterday.

"It's possible," said Essie. "I wish I could talk to someone who was there and might have seen her…"

"That would have been me," said the clerk. "I'm Phoebe, by the way. I see she was only here a short time, late yesterday afternoon. Hmmm. I think I remember her. Is she an older lady with light blond hair, rather short and curly?"

"Yes," cried Essie. The clerk's memory of the mysterious Carolyn was as good as hers. Of course, Phoebe had seen her in person and Essie had only seen her on the internet. "Can you remember anything about her? Do you remember anything about why she wanted to use the computer? Uh, because we all—I mean, her whole family—are just worried so much about her and wondering where she could be."

"Oh, my," said Phoebe, "I really wish I could help. Does she have dementia?"

"Why do you ask that?"

"Well, I mean, if she's wandered off on her own and no one knows where she is, I mean, that sounds a lot like dementia to me. I didn't mean to imply anything."

"Of course not," said Essie. "Actually, she doesn't have dementia—that I know of, but she is very upset."

"About what?" the clerk asked.

"Um," replied Essie, stumped. "Well, we're not all actually sure, but we're guessing that that may be one of the reasons she went to your center to use the computer. Also, she's been talking about Will a lot."

"Who's Will?" asked the clerk. *Well, that didn't help,* thought Essie. *I have no idea who he is and now I'll probably never find out.*

"Um, well we're not really sure, but she's been talking about someone named Will a lot lately," said Essie rather squeamishly.

"And you say she's not suffering from dementia?"

"Oh no."

"Okay, let me get this all straight, your sister is missing. She's been acting strangely lately, talking about someone named Will. She was here yesterday using our computers..."

"Yes," said Essie. "That's right."

"I, uh, don't think you ever told me how you knew your sister was here if she's missing."

"Um..." said Essie. *Oh great,* she thought. *Lying is so difficult.* Well, actually Carolyn did call me and she told me she'd been there but she didn't say where she was going afterward or where she went next..." *There, I think that covers all possibilities.*

"Hmm," said Phoebe, "well, I guess that sounds reasonable. I wish I could help you, Mrs. Cobb, did you say?"

"Yes," said Essie, "Jane Cobb. Thank you again. Good bye." She hung up abruptly, worrying that Phoebe was becoming suspicious. Well, it didn't matter. Essie thought she had acquired all of the information that she might possibly get from the woman. Actually, in retrospect, she'd probably gotten far more information than she could have normally expected, seeing as how she'd happened on the one person who had waited on Carolyn the previous day when she'd been at the Senior Center. And, best of all, she had a last name for Carolyn—Harper. Carolyn Harper from Bancroft Falls, New York. Next step—look her up and give her a call.

Calling down to the Happy Haven reception desk, Essie asked to again be connected to long distance in Bancroft Falls, New York.

"Information," said the operator.

"For what city?"

"Bancroft Falls, New York," said Essie.

"For what listing?"

"For Carolyn Harper," said Essie with a certain gleam in her voice.

"I have no listings for a Carolyn Harper in Bancroft Falls," said the voice.

"Any Harper with an initial C?"

"I'm looking. No, no Harper with the initial C either. I'm sorry."

"Oh, it's okay," said Essie. "It was a long shot."

"Pardon?"

"Thank you, operator," she said and hung up. *Well, back to Square One.*

Chapter 8

It was getting close to three o'clock and Essie had made certain that her computer was set up and plugged in. She had been to the restroom to comb her hair and powder her nose. The wonderful thing about the Zoom, she realized was that she only had to look nice from the neck up. She could wear her scruffy old sweat shirt and sweat pants and have her feet in her comfy slippers and no one would be the wiser as long as her hair was in place and her nose wasn't shiny. *Oh, isn't technology wonderful,* she sighed to herself.

It was only a few minutes to three. She was really excited because she knew Ned would be joining them and they had so many new things to share with each other. She would be able to reveal that she had discovered Carolyn's last name even though she hadn't been able to find a phone number for her in Bancroft Falls.

At three o'clock exactly, she pressed the host button on her screen that opened the Zoom app and invited the guests to join her on screen. She could see herself in her tiny box and she realized that her newly combed hair and newly powdered nose were hardly noticeable. Her efforts were probably to no avail but still she was glad she had made an attempt to look nice for her friends, just as she would have done if she had met them in the dining room.

"Hello. Is anyone there?" asked Essie, smiling for the camera.

A box opened and Fay joined in her own little box. Fay waved and pointed to the "Chat" box. Essie pressed it. "Hi, Essie," the note said.

"Hi, Fay," replied Essie and waved at her friend on the screen.

Another box popped open and Marjorie's lively face and shining red hair were visible.

"Hi, gals," she declared. "Fay, good to see you."

Fay waved back.

"Hi, Essie. I gave my night aide a package of hair products to give to your night aide."

"Hello, Marjorie. Thank you. I'll see what I can do with it." Opal's window appeared. "Hi, Opal."

"Hello, Essie, Marjorie, Fay," replied Opal.

"It's good to see you all," said Essie. "We're going to have a guest with us today."

"You mean you found Carolyn?" asked Opal.

"No, I wish," replied Essie. "But my grandson Ned is joining us. He's a sort of computer expert. It's his job and he's been giving me suggestions about…"

With that appropriate introduction, a new box appeared and Ned's face popped on the screen.

"Hello, ladies," he said. "I'm Ned. I'm Essie's grandson. Hope you don't mind my joining in."

"Are you kidding?" said Marjorie. "You're one of the few

actual males I've seen in ages."

"Marjorie," declared Opal. "He's Essie's grandson."

"It's okay, Miss Opal. If you don't mind the familiarity. I feel like I know you all as Grandma has told me all about you."

"She's obviously told you the most important information about Marjorie then," sneered Opal.

"And what would that be, Opal?" asked Marjorie.

"That you are man-crazy," replied Opal.

"I am not," cried Marjorie. "I'm just a normal woman with a normal interest in the opposite sex, unlike some old goats I might mention who act like they're too good..."

"Ladies," said Ned with a laugh, "no need to fight. I'm just an old married man with a child here to help you all out with your computer problem...and assist my favorite grandma in any way I can."

"See?" said Marjorie. Opal huffed and Fay clapped her hands together and smiled.

"Anyway, Ned," said Essie, trying to get the meeting back on track, "you have us all here. Where shall we start?"

"Well, ladies," said Ned, "why don't we start with you all telling me the situation with the mystery woman who appeared at your last Zoom meeting, and what you've done so far to locate her and then let's see what we can do next. Okay?"

"Okay," they all said—except Fay, of course, who gave her thumbs up sign.

"Well," said Essie, "as you know, this woman named Carolyn joined our Zoom meeting yesterday looking for someone named Will. She could see us and we could see her but she didn't seem to understand who we were or how she had landed in the middle of our meeting. She kept asking for Will and then eventually she disappeared. Fay tracked down her Zoom address and discovered she lived in Bancroft Falls, New

York."

"Good job on that, Fay," said Ned. "Some pretty fancy computing skills there."

Fay blushed and shook her head back and forth, causing her thick bangs to fluff out. Her chubby little cheeks wobbled when she moved her head.

"So Opal called the Bancroft Falls Senior Citizens' Center and talked to someone there but they couldn't give out personal information, they said," added Essie.

"That's still good," said Ned. "At least you know where she lives."

"And then," continued Essie, "I decided to be a bit devious this morning…"

"Oh, no, Essie, what did you do?" asked Opal.

"Oh, Opal," said Marjorie. "What horrible thing can she do from her living room?"

"Knowing Essie," replied Opal, "a lot."

"I guess your friends know you rather well, Grandma," said Ned, laughing.

"Anyway," said Essie, drawing out the word, "I called back to the Bancroft Falls Senior Citizens' Center a little bit ago and spoke with one of the clerks named Phoebe, who—it turned out—was the person who had helped Carolyn yesterday. She remembered her."

"And she just told you everything she knew about this Carolyn because you asked her? Some strange woman on the phone?" asked Opal.

"Well, not exactly," said Essie, scrunching her face together, "I did have to use a few little white lies—that my aide Joey suggested."

"Nice job, Essie," said Opal, "Blame poor Joey for your perfidy. As if he doesn't have enough problems without…"

"What problems?" asked Marjorie. "The poor boy. He's so nice. And so handsome."

"Ladies," called out Ned. "I think we're getting a bit side-tracked. Let's let Grandma finish her story—I mean her account—so we can see what we can do about this Carolyn... and then maybe we can take on your Joey's problems later..."

They all mumbled and Essie continued.

"Anyway," she said. "I made up a little story about Carolyn being my...uh, sister and told Phoebe. I said that she was missing and that we were trying to find her and that she had said she was going to the Senior Citizens' Center but that we didn't know where she was now and that the Senior Citizens' Center was the last place we knew for sure she had been."

"Very clever, Grandma," said Ned.

"Well, it worked...for a while. Phoebe told me what she could remember about Carolyn. Most important of all, she gave me the last name Carolyn used to sign in with at the Center—Harper. I tried to get other information, but unfortunately, I think Phoebe became suspicious."

"You mean that your lying skills aren't as fabulous as you'd like us to believe," said Marjorie.

"I challenge you to do any better, Marjorie."

"Ladies," yelled Ned again. "This is like refereeing a wrestling match. Continue, Grandma."

"I wanted to try to find out her address or phone number, but Phoebe started to get suspicious and wanted to know who I was, so I thought it was better to hang up while I was ahead."

"Wise move, Essie," said Opal. "You probably saved yourself from getting charged with fraud."

"I did not commit any fraud," cried Essie.

"Okay, okay," said Ned. "Let's stop and consider what information we have so far and what we need to do next. "We know pretty much for sure that our mystery lady is Carolyn Harper from Bancroft Falls, New York. Anyone want to dispute that?" He waited a bit. No one moved or spoke in their Zoom boxes.

"What else do we know?"

"We were discussing this, Ned," said Essie. "We obviously know that this Carolyn is at least mobile. She was able to get to the Senior Center on her own so she either drove there, had someone take her there, or took a cab."

"I vote for drove there," said Marjorie. "If someone brought her, she would have to contact the person to pick her up. The same for a cab. If she drove, she would just arrive and then leave when she finished. I take it this Phoebe didn't say anything about her waiting around for a ride?"

"No," said Essie, "but then, once she started becoming suspicious of me, I fear she was more and more reluctant to give me any information."

"That's okay," said Ned. "I don't really think it matters how she arrived at the center. Does anyone have any more information that might help?"

Fay raised her hand and pointed to the "Chat" box. They all clicked on the box and a link to the Bancroft Falls Hometown Site popped up.

"Fay," said Ned, "this is great. I see there's a map here. We can get an idea of the size of Carolyn's community. It says it has a population of about 40,000. That's not huge but it's still pretty big. We obviously can't go there so we need to figure this out from a distance. Oh, look. There's a map of the city—there's the downtown area. Let me just focus in and see if I can find the….Oh, yes. There it is. The Bancroft Falls Senior Citizens' Center. On the corner of Westmore and Hart, in the middle of their downtown area. Looks like it's also within walking distance of some very residential areas too, so it's possible that our Carolyn actually walked to the Center and walked back home. Unfortunately, we don't know her address, so we don't know if she even could walk there or if she had to have driven."

"So Ned," said Essie, "what do you suggest we do next?"

"Hmm," said Ned. "Let me ask Fay. Fay, you seem to have some remarkable search skills. I would do this myself if I didn't have to get to a meeting in a few minutes, but I'm wondering if you could track down a telephone directory for Bancroft Falls, New York, extract the listings for all the Harpers and then forward them to your compatriots in Happy Haven. Actually, it would be best to divide the list of Harpers into fourths and give a fourth..."

"Ned," said Essie, "I see what you're going to suggest. Let's let Fay do the searching for the phone numbers but have her divide them into thirds and send a third each to me, Opal, and Marjorie."

"Oh, of course," replied Ned, now realizing that Fay's skills did not extend to vocal interaction. "Then each of the three of you, call the Harpers on your list and see if you can find Carolyn. Surely she didn't give the wrong last name. Why would she? We were the ones trying to pull a fast one, so to speak. She's just trying to track down this Will. And we just want to help her. Remember that. Ultimately, we don't want to cause her any trouble."

"Of course, Ned," said Essie. "Are we all okay?"

Fay waved her hand. They all looked at the "Chat." Fay had written "I have no way to send printed version of the phone numbers."

Ned said, "Let me take care of that part, Fay. You send the complete list to my email address here (he typed his email address into the chat box) and I'll see that it's divided, printed and delivered to all three of the ladies tomorrow. How's that?"

"Oh, Ned, that's the cow's blouse," said Essie. "I promise I will start calling Harpers the minute I get the list."

"Great, ladies. And let's not let the fact that we have a specific job to do keep us from thinking outside the box as I know all of you are capable of doing. Let's keep working to help Carolyn. Okay?"

"For Carolyn," said Essie.

"For Carolyn," added Opal and Marjorie. Fay gave her thumbs up in reply.

"Then I will keep in touch through Grandma and if any of you need anything from me, just let her know. Bye, ladies." Ned's square disappeared.

"Wow," said Essie. "I feel like we accomplished a lot."

"I do too," said Marjorie. "Essie, your grandson is really cute."

"Marjorie," cried Essie.

"Oh, give up, Essie," said Opal. "She's hopeless." They all laughed and hung up.

Chapter 9

That night Essie's aide Clarice brought the hair products that Marjorie had promised and the two of them attempted to wind her hair around the little plastic foam rollers after her shower and hair washing. They concluded by putting on the little fancy cloth cap that Marjorie had included in the package. Essie tried to sleep with the foreign objects all over her head but it was very difficult.

In the morning, she did as Marjorie had instructed the aide to tell her to do. She gently removed the rollers and fluffed out her sparkling white curls.

"Roast ghost," she cried as she stared at herself in the mirror. "My hair does look remarkably better. Well, I'll be. I'll have to tell Marjorie that she was right about something. That will not be pleasant." Even so, Essie smiled back at herself in the mirror, and then headed out to her living room.

She rolled her walker over to the window. Red was there. He seemed to be waiting for her on a branch of the evergreen tree when she opened her blinds.

She had just settled in her recliner when Joey popped his head in the door.

"Hey, Miss Essie," he called out. "My, you look lovely today."

"Thank you. New hair treatment thanks to my friend Marjorie. How are you this very sunny morning, Joey?"

"I'm okay," he replied. He set down her tray on the kitchen counter and quickly did her temperature check. Then he brought her tray over to her and placed it gently on her hassock.

"What's this?" said Essie, noting a large brown paper envelope with a stick-on label pasted to the front.

"That was in your mail box this morning," he said. "You usually don't get mail until the postman comes in the afternoon, but this came by courier and was addressed to you so I brought it up."

"Oh, it must be the printed list of addresses for all the Harpers in Bancroft Falls, New York."

"The what?" asked Joey.

"Oh, I guess you haven't heard the latest," said Essie, as she pried open the top of the flap and pulled out a few pages of the Bancroft Falls' telephone directory. It listed names, addresses and phone numbers for all the Harpers in the town. As she glanced at the number of individuals on the pages, she realized that there weren't as many as she had originally assumed there would be. Ned had thoughtfully had his secretary produce the lists in large print. There were probably about twenty names per sheet and there were three sheets altogether. "Remember that lady who popped in on our Zoom meeting the other day? Well, we managed to find out her name and now we're trying to track her down and contact her so we can find out how to help her find Will. These are lists of all the people in her town with her last name."

"Wow," said Joey. "You and your friends are very resourceful."

"Well, my grandson helped. And so did you, Joey. You helped us get coordinated on our computers. We couldn't have done it without you. And you did sort of hint to me that I might need to tell a fib or two to get information from that Senior Center…"

"And did you?"

"I may have said a falsehood or two," she said sweetly, with a big smile.

"Miss Essie, you are quite a gal."

"Joey, do you know if Marjorie and Opal got packages like this or was I the only one?"

"I don't think they did, Miss Essie. I can see everyone's boxes when I go in the back room and this was the only envelope in a box this morning."

"Then this must be the entire list. Now that I glance at it, it would have to be, as all the Harpers on these lists run from an Abraham Harper to a Wendell Harper. I guess Ned had his secretary divide them up into three even sheets, one for each of us."

"I have to take Miss Opal her breakfast in a bit. Do you want me to bring her one of the sheets?"

"That would be great. Could you take the third one over to Marjorie in 226 when you have time?"

"Sure. So I assume you ladies are going to be spending your day today calling all these people named Harper in this small town and try to track down this Carolyn?"

"That's the plan, Joey. I know it sounds boring, but surely with the three of us on it, we'll find her. We just want to help her. Our intentions are good."

"Oh, Miss Essie, I know that. Let me know if there's

anything else I can do to help you." With that, he picked up the two address sheets that Essie was not holding and headed out.

While Essie was drinking her coffee and finishing off her toast, the phone rang.

"Hi, Grandma," she heard Ned's cheery voice ring out. "Did you get the address lists I sent?"

"I did, Ned, and I already sent Joey off with two of them to give to Opal and Marjorie and I have the third one. I'll start calling the names on this list today and see what I find out," she said.

"Great," he said. "Grandma, I was thinking, well—er, wondering just what you're going to say to these people when you call. You aren't going to use that fake story you gave when you called the Senior Center about your sister being missing, are you?"

"I don't know. I haven't thought about it. It seemed like a good plan."

"But, Grandma, think about it. When and if you reach the Harper you're looking for, you can't claim you're that person's sister. What if you get someone on the line who knows your Carolyn and you claim to be her sister and this person knows she doesn't have a sister, say?"

"Hmm. I see what you mean. You're right, Ned. I'll have to think this through more carefully. Do you think the best way is to just tell each person exactly what happened in the Zoom meeting and why I'm calling."

"Truthfully, Grandma, I think truth may be the best course."

"There's a lot of truth in that, Ned." Essie chuckled.

"That's the truth."

"Oh, stop," she said. "I'll think about it. But you know me, I'm really good with a nice fancy lie…"

"Yes, and you've gotten in a lot of trouble with those fancy lies too," he reminded her. "Well, whatever you do, I support you. Just let me know if I can do anything else…"

"Actually, Ned, there was one other thing. I don't really know if this is something you can help with, but I know the internet has more answers and solutions than I am—or ever could be—aware of, so I'm hoping you might suggest something…"

"I'll try, Grandma," he said. "What is it?"

"My aide Joey," she began. "He's working here temporarily. I think he might even be in computer stuff like you but he moved back home recently to live with his parents who own a small restaurant here in Reardon that is really struggling during this pandemic. I think Joey gives them all of his earnings from working here at Happy Haven which wouldn't be much. I know he's terribly worried about them and he's been wonderful to me…and in helping us with tracking down Carolyn."

"Hmm," said Ned, musing. "You're right when you say there are answers on the internet that we may have never thought of before, and I actually think there may be a solution for Joey and his family that we—and by we, I mean I—could set up, but that you and your lady friends would have to do most of the work on…"

"Oh, we would, Ned. Every one of us love Joey."

"Good. There are various internet sites that fund different groups or organizations or even just individual people like Joey who have worthy goals. Someone sets up a fund for this person or group and then other people on the internet contribute if they want to, based on how worthy they think the goal is and whether they really want to help the person."

"That sounds wonderful, Ned."

"How about I set up a fund for Joey's family restaurant? I'll take care of everything at the Internet end. You and your pals will need to provide me with information—anything you can find about Joey, his parents, the restaurant, will be ideal. Oh, and photos. We'll need to get a photo of Joey, preferably with you and the other ladies. Get a photo of his restaurant too. Fay can probably research the restaurant and…when is your next Zoom meeting?"

"I hadn't thought about it, but I guess we can keep doing one each day at three p.m."

"That would be perfect. I have an idea for today's meeting. Can you get Joey to be at your apartment for the start of it? Or he could be at one of the other lady's places."

"Of course, Ned. That won't be hard. I know he gets off at three, so I can probably get him to stop by here before he heads home. But if you're thinking of getting a photo of him, I should warn you that he's always wearing his pandemic space suit. He won't take it off for anything; it's the rules."

"Okay. I think that'll be okay; it'll just emphasize how dire the situation is and why the family restaurant is having so much trouble. Believe me, Joey's family is not alone in this."

"Oh, I know, but I know Joey, and he's like a member of my family and it hurts me to see him in pain."

"Then, we're going to do something for him, Grandma. For both Joey and Carolyn. You really are trying to solve problems in the world."

"No, I can't do that, just a few that are in my little corner of it."

"Okay, Grandma. I hear you. I'll see you this afternoon. In the meantime, get busy on your list of Harpers—and let's keep to the truth this time."

"Yes, Ned," replied Essie in her most polite voice.

The two hung up their phones.

"Hmm," mused Essie. "The truth? Well, it might work."

Chapter 10

Essie spent the morning with her list of people named Harper in Bancroft Falls, New York. At one point in making her calls, she realized that she was racking up quite a few long distance calls. That would make her phone bill much higher next month. Pru, who always helped her do her bills each month, would surely wonder about all these calls to a little town in New York State. *Oh, well, I can't worry about it now,* she thought. *I just have to get on with my task.*

She started at the top of the list. Her list had Harpers with first names starting with A's through L's. She'd given Opal the M's through R's, and Marjorie S's through Z's. Her first call was to Abraham Harper.

"Hello, may I speak to Abraham Harper?" she asked the brusque-sounding gentleman who answered.

"You got him," said the man.

"Oh, good morning, Mr. Harper," said Essie in her sweetest voice. "My name is Essie Cobb and I'm calling from…"

"Don't want any…" said the man.

"Oh, I'm not a salesperson," said Essie quickly, jumping in. "I'm calling from the Happy Haven Assisted Living Facility. I'm a resident. I was participating in a Zoom meeting yesterday and this lady who I didn't know appeared on my screen…"

"What's that got to do with me?" barked the man.

"Well, maybe nothing," said Essie, "but please hear me out. This lady we found out later is named Carolyn Harper and we also found out she's from Bancroft Falls. Do you know her?"

"No," he said.

"I mean," continued Essie, "maybe she's a cousin or something."

"She's not. I don't know her. Good bye." He hung up.

Well, said Essie to herself, *that was rude.* She went on to the next person on her list: A. E. Harper. She dialed the number. No answer. *Not unusual,* she thought, listening to the steady rings. Like many if not most of the numbers in the directory, this was probably a landline number, and Essie had learned that many people no longer had landline telephones. Even if they did, they used their cellphones more often. *How depressing*, she thought. She looked at the list and wondered if they'd ever be able to track down Carolyn Harper and find out if she had found Will. Finally, she gave up waiting for an answer and hung up. She placed a question mark by A. E. Harper's name (She had already crossed out Abraham Harper's name).

The next name on her list was Benjamin Harper. She rang the number. She was about ready to give up when a frazzled-sounding young woman answered.

"Hello?" Essie could hear a baby crying in the background.

"Hello? Is Benjamin Harper there?"

"He's not here now. This is his wife. Can I help you?"

"Hello, Mrs. Harper. My name is Essie Cobb. I'm calling you from the Happy Haven Assisted Living Facility. I was in a

Zoom meeting yesterday when a lady named Carolyn Harper appeared. She was very distraught and she was looking for someone named Will. We tried to help her but she seemed confused. She left the meeting and we later learned she lives in Bancroft Falls. I'm wondering if she might be related to you or your husband."

"Carolyn?" repeated the woman, the baby still crying. "I don't think Ben has any relatives named Carolyn. No one who lives here in town, anyway. He might have some cousins further upstate, but I don't remember their names. The only female relative he has in town is his mom and her name is Pixie. I know. Silly name for a woman, but she's really nice."

"She sounds lovely," said Essie, now anxious to extract herself from this conversation and move on to the next name. "Well, if you discover that Carolyn is a relative, please call me." She gave the woman her number and hung up. She marked her list with a question mark and moved on to the next number. This one was Carl E. Harper. She dialed and an answering machine responded with a woman's voice. "I can't come to the phone. Please leave a message and I will return your call later." Essie did as the voice directed, leaving her contact information, then hanging up, and putting a question mark by the name of Carl E. Harper on her list.

Next on the list was Charles Harper. Essie was getting the hang of the routine now. She placed the call, and luckily got an actual person this time.

"Hello," said a male voice.

"Is this Charles Harper?"

"It is. What can I do for you?"

Essie explained her dilemma and Charles Harper turned out to be a very sympathetic gentleman who was interested in his fellow citizens and their dilemmas. He tried to think of all of the people he knew in Bancroft Falls with his last name who might be——or even be related to——the lady Essie was searching for. In fact, he and Essie had such a connection that it was almost as if he was joining in with her to help find the missing Carolyn. But in the end, he had to admit that he simply didn't know the lady or have any idea who she might be or how to find her in Bancroft Falls. Essie hung up feeling like her one good lead had fallen through. Then, she chastised herself.

"That wasn't a lead, Essie," she said out loud. "That was just you getting your hopes up."

Back to the list. The morning was pretty much gone by then. Essie had only gotten through a handful of names. She counted the remaining names. She had twelve to go. This would never do. She'd really have to speed things up. She called the next one which turned out to be a disconnected number and she marked it as such on her list. The next call got her a voice message and she left what was becoming her now standard recording. She tried really hard to get through at least half the list before lunch. She knew she'd only have a few hours after lunch to make the rest of the calls as their Zoom meeting was scheduled for three p.m. and she couldn't miss that. But, she really wanted to be able to report something at the meeting—something more than just that she'd called twenty or so Harpers in Bancroft Falls. Just as she finished up her next call—number thirteen, auspiciously, Joey entered with her lunch. Before he could speak, Essie was struck with a sense that she was forgetting something—or remembering something—but she couldn't quite tell which one it was.

Chapter 11

"Oh, Joey," she cried as she hung up the phone. "Don't tell me it's lunch time already."

"Sure is, Miss Essie," said her spaceman attendant as he brought over the tray and placed it on her footstool. "How are you coming along with your phoning? Have you found your Carolyn yet?"

"No such luck," she replied. "I wonder how Opal and Marjorie are doing. Better than me, I hope." She put down her list and her pen and set her tray on her lap and started to dig into a plate of spaghetti. "Yum, spaghetti."

"Seems you've got your appetite back, Miss Essie," observed Joey. "Must be because you have a 'case' to work on."

"I think so, Joey. And it seems to me that you must run from one apartment to another. Do you ever get an opportunity to sit down and catch your breath? Grab a bite?"

"Of course," he replied. "Actually, I like to keep busy. No time to worry then. I'm usually up by five and I get here to Happy Haven around six. Once I leave here, I rush home and immediately start helping my folks at the restaurant."

"Are you a cook?" she asked.

"Oh, no," he laughed.

"A waiter?"

"No, I'm delivery. You know that's about all we can do these days. They're not allowing indoor dining now, so all our business comes from take-out or delivery. I spend my evenings carting pizzas around to people all over town in my mini-van." Joey smiled but Essie could see the sadness behind his eyes.

"Do your parents cook?" she asked.

"My dad's the cook and my mom runs the business side. We used to have about twenty employees but they're all gone now. No jobs for them. I'm the only one they have working for them and, of course, they don't pay me. I give them everything I earn here at Happy Haven too, but I get free room and board so it's a fair trade. Even if I didn't, I'd work for them for free during this pandemic. The thought of my family's restaurant going under breaks my heart; it's been here in town for over fifty years, passed down from my Dad's father and grandfather— Rizzoli's."

"So, you're Joey Rizzoli."

"Yup, Italian through and through. We don't give up."

"That's amazing, Joey," Essie said. "Are you getting any aid from the government?"

"Not enough to really help," he said. "If we can't get back to indoor seating pretty soon, I'm afraid we're going to have to…" He stopped and stared out Essie's one living room window at the evergreen trees and bushes. "Sorry, Miss Essie, you don't want to hear this."

"Actually, Joey, I do," she said. "It's good for me to realize how truly blessed I am to be living here at Happy Haven, protected and safe, and knowing that my family is doing okay too. I can't bear thinking that someone who has come to mean so much to me—like you, Joey—is having so much trouble."

"I appreciate that, Miss Essie," he said. "But right now, as it looks like you've scarfed down that spaghetti, I'm going to save myself a few steps and take your tray with me. Okay?"

"Oh, one other thing," she said.

"Anything," he replied, stopping in the doorway.

"Would you be able to stop by here at three or a little after? The Zoom group has something they want to ask you?"

"Really?" he said, chuckling. "Something they want to ask me? Sounds intriguing. Of course, I'll pop by before I sign out and then see what all you gals are up to and what I can do for you Zoomers."

"Great," said Essie. "See you at three or shortly thereafter."

After Joey had left, Essie quickly returned to her long distance calling. She was now into the H's so her next call went to Harold J. Harper. Mr. Harper was busy or unavailable according to his voice mail, and Essie was forced to leave a voice message, which she did. She notated this on her list and went on to James E. Harper who turned out to be disconnected according to the phone company. She marked that too. Really, were any people with telephones actually home and answering them? Next up was Lawrence Harper. With this number, Essie again connected with Mr. Harper's wife who assured her that he had no relative named Carolyn. She drew a line through his name on her list. Essie made several more calls but the results were similar to the previous ones. No one she actually spoke with indicated in any way that they had a relative named Carolyn Harper or that they even knew anyone named Carolyn Harper. It was all negative news—but it was news. They at least could eliminate people from the list. She only hoped that Opal or Marjorie would have better luck.

As she finished up her last call, she glanced down at her wristwatch and realized that it was time for her to start getting ready for the Zoom meeting. She scuttled into her bathroom and did some ablutions. She puffed her nose powder and used her brush to fluff her new head of shiny curls. Everything looked neat enough for the little built-in camera on the computer, she surmised. She headed back to the living room and sat down on her sofa in front of her computer. She plugged the laptop in and turned on all of the buttons she knew she had to press to get the machine up and working. Soon, her Zoom screen appeared and she could see her image in the little box on the screen. She smiled at herself and checked her watch. Three o'clock on the nose. Time to start.

Chapter 12

When Essie logged onto her Zoom screen, she saw a red light blinking. Mystified, she clicked into the Zoom program and discovered that Ned was already there in his little box.

"Hi, Grandma. I wanted to get here early and get things set up."

"What things?" she asked.

"Oh, just some buttons and knobs I need to press so I can get the information and photos I'll need when everyone arrives."

At that moment, there was a knock on Essie's door and Joey popped his head in.

"Hey, Miss Essie," he called out in a loud whisper when he saw her sitting in front of her computer talking to someone.

"Hi, Joey," she called to him. "Come on over and meet my grandson, Ned."

Joey bounded over to the sofa, trying not to let the flying wings of his disinfected suit bump into any of Essie's lamps or knickknacks. Essie turned the screen towards Joey and Ned greeted him.

Wow," said Ned. "I see what you mean, Grandma. You really can't see what he looks like with all that stuff covering him."

"It's for safety," said Joey, "your grandmother's, as well as mine." He stood there, obviously unsure of himself and just what he was supposed to do.

"It's fine, Joey," said Essie, patting his arm.

"Yeah, Joe," said Ned. "It's fine. No worries. Hey, can you open my grandma's living room blinds, a bit?"

"Sure," said Joey, striding over and adjusting the blinds so more afternoon sunlight seeped through and lit up the screen. "Look, Miss Essie, a cardinal."

"That's Red. He's my special pal."

"He seems friendly. Maybe he wants to join the Zoom meeting," suggested Joey, returning to the sofa.

Back at the computer screen, Marjorie's box opened and Marjorie greeted Essie.

"Oh, Essie, you must have used those curlers I sent you. Your hair looks wonderful."

"Thank you, Marjorie. I did use them and it was fairly easy. Thank you again for sending them."

"You're welcome." Marjorie could obviously see movement behind Essie. "What's going on?" she asked.

"Ned is fixing the lighting in my room or something," she replied. "I don' really know. Joey is here, Marjorie."

"Oh, Joey. How are you?" said Marjorie through the screen in her most beguiling voice, eyelashes fluttering.

"Really, Marjorie," scolded Essie.

"Okay," said Ned. "Let's get everyone together."

Two more squares popped open and Fay and Opal appeared on the screen.

"Essie, your hair looks so nice. What did you do to it?" asked Opal.

"Marjorie's curlers," said Essie. "I'm so glad. Now I don't look like I've been electrocuted."

"Okay, Grandma," said Ned. "I'm all set. Thanks, Joey."

"You're welcome," Joey replied to the laptop.

"Everyone is here, Ned. What do you need us to do?" asked Essie.

"Okay, everyone," said Ned. "I asked Grandma if I could join your group today for a little experiment. I hope you all don't mind. I've got this new internet camera feature that I've been wanting to try out and now that I have a disparate group like yours, I can play around with some of its features..."

Essie looked at her friends and realized that they all had strange looks on their faces. This wasn't what they were expecting, but seeing as how Joey was there and everyone could see him, Essie was not going to say anything about how any of this pertained to helping him and his family's restaurant.

"Okay," said Ned again. "What I need you all to do is just smile nicely right into your cameras." They all did.

"What about me, Ned? And Joey?"

"Yes, Grandma, that's why I asked you to have someone join you. I want to see if this camera will work with two people in the shot. Can you bend down, Joey, and you and Grandma put your heads together. Great. Just like that."

Joey bent over and he and Essie stared at the camera.

Very clever, thought Essie. *Joey will never guess that we're doing all of this because of him. Good job, Ned.*

"It would really help if you could take off your helmet, Joe— just for a bit."

"Sorry. I just can't do that," said Joey.

"Okay. I understand. How about you turn just a bit to your right so there isn't so much glare on your face." Joey followed directions. "Great. Now it's almost as if there isn't any plastic there at all. Great. Everyone hold." They all held. Ned pressed some buttons and then said, "That's it. Folks, thank you so much. I'm going to go see how this all prints out now. Sorry to spoil your meeting. Joey, you're finished too. I bet you'd like to get out of there."

"Yes, my parents are expecting me home. Bye, ladies," he said to the women on the screen and Essie as he headed out the door.

As soon as he'd left, Essie said, "Ned, he's gone. Did you really get what you need? And, can you tell us what it is you needed? What is it you've planned?"

"Are you sure he's gone, Grandma?"

"Yes, he's gone," she replied.

"Okay," said Ned. "I was being honest with Joey. I was taking photos of him and you, Grandma—and all of you. Ladies, what I'm going to do is set up a funding page for Joey on the internet. People will come visit this page and learn about how wonderful he is there at Happy Haven and also how hard he's working to help his parents save their restaurant, then hopefully, they will be motivated to donate money to this funding page. This is part of a site called "Save Me." There are all sorts of projects on it but all of them are worthy—and believe me, ladies, with the pandemic, the number of projects on "Save Me" has increased dramatically."

"That's wonderful," said Marjorie.

"What can we do to help?" asked Opal.

"I'm going to take care of the technical end; that part won't be hard for me. What I need from you all is information—about Joey and his family and their restaurant. I suggest that Fay be in charge of finding photographs of the restaurant and the family online. Grandma, you and Marjorie, and Opal, find out everything you can about Joey—his life, his history, his family.

I particularly need to know what sort of financial hardships he has. Like if he has a large student loan or any such thing. Opal, since you were in the business world, maybe you can look into his parents' restaurant and see what their financial situation is. Now that's something I don't know anything about or how to find it. I doubt we would want to reveal their debt on the site, but it would be helpful for us to know so we know how much money we have to raise."

"I can do that," said Opal. "I know several people I can contact who can help me and they're all discreet."

"Great," said Ned. "I think that's all as far as setting up Joey's Save Me page. Once I get it going and you send me——"

"Where should we send this information, Ned?" asked Marjorie coyly.

"Oh, if it's concrete, have an aide—not Joey—bring it to Grandma, and she and I will figure out how to get it to me."

"That sounds good, Ned," said Essie.

"Now, what about your lady Carolyn?" Ned asked. "Any updates?"

"We haven't had any chance to discuss among ourselves yet about our progress," said Essie. "I will report to you all that I called all of the Harpers on my list today but didn't locate Carolyn. Very disappointing——although there were some numbers where I got an answering machine and I left my name and phone number."

"I had the same experience," reported Opal. "I finished the list faster than I thought I would because so many numbers just never answered or had answering machines. I'll go back tomorrow and call the numbers that didn't answer but I'm not terribly hopeful."

"I wish I could say that my experience was better," added Marjorie, "but it was pretty much the same as Essie's and

Opal's. I really thought we'd found our Carolyn, but if she lives in Bancroft Falls, New York, and has a telephone, I don't think she's in the phonebook."

"She probably has a cell phone like most people these days," said Ned. "Grandma, I don't suppose you could call back to that lady at the Senior Center and pump her for more information on Carolyn, could you?"

"What would I ask?"

"I'm wondering if when Carolyn signed in, her name was all she was required to give. I mean when I sign in to all sorts of places, I have to give name, phone number, sometimes address. What's really strange to me is that not one person on those lists whom you spoke to had ever even heard of her. Is she some sort of recluse? We've already discussed her mobility. She must have driven to the center or possibly walked as it looked from the map Fay showed us yesterday that the center is fairly close to lots of side streets. I can see her being frightened by something, and running down to the center where she might think she would get help and then becoming frustrated when she lands in a Zoom meeting with the four of you."

"Yes, we'd frustrate anyone," said Opal, glumly.

"Oh, Opal," said Essie. "That's no attitude."

"Now, ladies," said Ned. "Don't become discouraged. Grandma, this is a mystery. And you are the queen of solving mysteries as far as I'm concerned. I feel hopeful that we'll figure this out if we all work together and share information. If any of you has any ideas about how we might track down Carolyn, share it with all of us. Fay and I can track information on the internet and the rest of you can make phone calls. I think that covers all the bases as far as discovering what we need to know about this unknown lady."

"I agree," said Essie. "Ned, with all of us working together and sharing our information and ideas, I'm sure we can find Carolyn and figure out how we can help her."

"Before it's too late," added Opal.

Chapter 13

As soon as the Zoom group disbanded, Essie lost no time in making a phone call. This time it was a repeat call. She contacted the long distance operator on her landline phone and made another call to the Bancroft Falls Senior Citizens' Center.

"Bancroft Falls Senior Citizens' Center," said a male voice when the operator connected her.

"Oh, hello," said Essie. "I was wondering if Phoebe was there."

"Sorry, she's left for the day," said the cheerful gentleman. "Can I help you?"

"Maybe," said Essie. "I was speaking to her yesterday and I'm afraid I may have led her astray."

"Oh?" said the man. "How so?"

"Well, maybe I'll just tell you the story and you can decide for yourself if you want to help me or not."

"Sounds fair," he said.

"I'm Essie, by the way," she said. "Essie Cobb. I live in the Happy Haven Assisted Living Facility."

"So, you're in our demographic," replied the man.

"Yes."

"Glad to meet you, Essie," he said. "I'm Phillip George. I'm a retired volunteer—one of three volunteers who work here. You spoke with Phoebe, I guess, already. So what can I do for you?"

"Okay, here goes," said Essie. "Phillip, I'm afraid I lied to Phoebe yesterday when I talked to her."

"Well, that's an admission. I take it you plan to tell me the truth?"

"Yes, and I totally understand if you don't want to talk to me, or if you'd like to contact Phoebe or even wait until you see her again. Do you two ever share the same schedules?"

"Yes, our schedules overlap quite a bit," he replied. "Before we worry about how we might punish you, Essie, why don't you just tell me how you lied to Phoebe and how I might help you."

"Okay," said Essie. "You're very kind. Several days ago my friends and I were participating in a Zoom meeting. We can't get together in person here at the Happy Haven Assisted Living Facility because of the pandemic..."

"Oh, I know what you're going through," injected Phillip. "I've got my mask on as we speak."

"Anyway, my girlfriends and I were just having a pleasant conversation over Zoom when all of a sudden, a lady named Carolyn whom we didn't recognize popped up in a box on our Zoom screen and started asking who we were and then she started asking where Will was,"

"Will who?"

"We don't know," said Essie, "but that's what she was saying, 'Where's Will?' And then she said something like 'He said Will would be here.' I had no idea who this lady was or who Will was and neither did any of my friends on Zoom. And then almost as soon as Carolyn appeared, she disappeared and all of us were left feeling totally mystified. And more than that, we all felt worried for this woman and we all decided then and there that we had to do something to help her find her Will. The first thing we did was trace the Zoom ID she'd used to enter our chat room. That listed your address—the Bancroft Falls Senior Citizens' Center. We weren't sure what to do next, but we got the phone number for your center and when my friend Opal called and asked about tracing the name of this Carolyn who had used your computer and had somehow gotten on our Zoom call accidentally, she was immediately told that it was against your policy to give out information about your members."

"That would have been me," said Phil. "I remember your friend's call and I remember saying that."

"Anyway," continued Essie, "the next day I called and got Phoebe and instead of telling her the truth that I have just told to you, I am embarrassed to say that I made up a story because I thought it might be more effective."

"Oh," said Phil. "Or because you thought Phoebe might be more likely to fall for a lie than I had been?"

"Yes, to be honest."

"Well, that's what you say you're being now, right?"

"Yes," agreed Essie. "Has it worked?"

"I'm still on the line."

"Anyway, the only information I got out of Phoebe—and believe me it was difficult—was that someone named Carolyn Harper had used your computers about the time that we held our Zoom meeting. I tried to get more information such as her address or phone number or something, but Phoebe wouldn't give me that. Truly, she didn't even realize she'd given me Carolyn's last name because I'd woven such an elaborate tale, but I won't go into all that." Essie coughed in embarrassment.

"No, I don't think you need to do that," agreed Phil, "but it seems that you're still following up on this—in the more honest and truthful way that you're now doing—because you are genuinely worried about this Carolyn Harper and her welfare. Am I right?"

"That's it," cried Essie. "We're not trying to scam anyone. We want to find Carolyn and help her find Will. Can you help us? I know it's against your policy but isn't there some way you can at least steer me in the right direction so we can help this poor lady? I mean, she's a constituent of yours and I'd think you'd want to help her."

"Well, I suppose I can try," said Phil, "but I genuinely don't know what other information I could give you that might help you track down your Carolyn other than what you have already."

"Do you keep records of the people who use your Center?"

"Well, we do check their Medicare or Social Security cards when they come in, just to prove that they are seniors and have the right to use our Center for free."

"So if Carolyn was there using your computers, that means she had already been admitted and we know she's a senior."

"That would be true," he said.

"What about transportation?" Essie asked. "I mean, how do people get to your facility?"

"All sorts of ways. We're sort of on the outskirts of our town's downtown sector. We're surrounded by residential areas. Lots of seniors just walk in. There's a bus stop a block away. Some might take the bus here. Others who can still drive would park in our parking lot or have someone drop them off. I would have no way of knowing how Carolyn got here or how she left."

"I know you can't officially tell me, but do you have any

record of Carolyn other than her first and last name and that she's officially a senior citizen? I mean, what about an address? We got a list of all the Harpers in Bancroft Falls and called every one of them, and still couldn't find her."

"Wow. You women are serious about this," he said.

"Yes, we are. We're going to do whatever we can to find Carolyn and help her find Will. We just need a little bit of help from somewhere else." Essie sighed so deeply she almost felt as if she might cry.

"Essie, can you describe what Carolyn looks like?"

"Well, those Zoom boxes are fairly small, but I think I can. She was elderly, and she had fluffy, straw-colored hair. And of course, she was visibly upset."

"Hang on a minute, Essie," said Phil. She waited. After a few minutes, he returned, "Essie, you there?"

"I'm here."

"I've got Gloria here. She mans the front desk in the afternoons. She was working the day that your Carolyn Harper came in. I described her to Gloria, and Gloria says she thinks she remembers her. Here, I'll let you talk to her." There was the sound of the receiver being handed from one person to another.

"Hello," said a sprightly voice. "I'm Gloria. How can I help?"

"Hello, I'm Essie. Your Phil says you might remember the lady I'm looking for. Her name is Carolyn Harper. She came in the other afternoon?"

"Yes," replied Gloria. "I think I know the lady you mean, if you mean the one who was almost frantic with worry. She had never been here before and she walked in…"

"Did you see her drive up in a car?"

"No, as a matter of fact, I saw her walking down the street from the north. So, that would mean she didn't take the bus, because if she did, then she would have been walking from the south. When she came in, she was shaking. I think she might have been crying. It looked as if she might even have run some of the way to get to us."

"That's very helpful, Gloria. What else do you remember? Did she say why she was so upset?"

"It was something about someone named Will. She kept repeating something to herself like, 'Oh, Will. I hope you're okay. Please, please be okay.' And things like that."

"Did you get the impression that Will was sick?"

"I don't know—either that or in serious trouble," replied Gloria. "I remember asking her if I could help her and she just said, 'I need to use your computer,' so I sent her to the back room where we keep our computers. Phil can tell you about that end."

"Thanks, Gloria. If you think of anything else—anything at all—that might help us track Carolyn down and help her find Will, please contact me." Essie gave Gloria her telephone number and then spoke again to Phil.

"Thank you, Phil," said Essie. "This is really helpful. I think it shows me that Carolyn lives somewhere within walking distance of your center. Do you remember anything about what she did on the computer? Did she know what she was doing? Anything?"

"No, I'm really sorry," said Phil. "She went to the computer and signed in and then began typing. She didn't ask for any help so I didn't stick around to assist her. If I remember correctly, she hardly stayed but a few minutes, then she got up, grabbed her belongings and stormed out."

"Yes, that would coincide with the experience we went through with her on our Zoom meeting," said Essie. "Well, I can't think of any more questions to ask you, Phil. But may I leave my phone number with you? If you think of anything at all related to Carolyn, would you please call me?"

"Of course, I'd be happy to."

"And, if perchance, Carolyn Harper returns to your center, would you please give that number to her and make sure she calls me?"

"I will certainly do my best."

"Thank you so much."

"Best of luck," said Phil. "I certainly hope you solve the problem and can help Carolyn find her Will."

They hung up.

Chapter 14

That night Essie tossed and turned in her bed. She was thinking about Carolyn. In her dream, she saw her—a thin lady with very fine wispy hair. She was running down the street in what Essie imaged was Bancroft Falls, searching for her Will and crying out his name. She was reaching out, trying to grasp something. Essie felt like whatever Carolyn was reaching for was something she needed and it was just beyond her fingertips. What was it? Was it something she'd forgotten? Was it a clue that she hadn't yet unraveled? She thought and thought about all the events of the last few days—about the abrupt start of this whole puzzle when Carolyn had burst into their Zoom session. About her crying out for Will, and then her even more abrupt departure. And about how they were all mystified by Carolyn's problem and what they could do to help. Essie wondered if they had considered every possible avenue to try to find her. Was there some other way they could try to track down the missing woman? Why did she feel as if she'd just missed connecting some important piece of the puzzle?

In the morning, Essie took her time getting dressed and ready for her day. The only positive note was the fact that her head was covered in curls that were still tight and shiny. They had stayed in place while she had slept. *Thank you, Marjorie,* she thought. She thought again about her dream and wondered if it provided any clues for how to contact the missing Carolyn. She wandered out to her living room and pushed her walker over to her window. Unlike her dark mood, the outside was sunny, and rays were streaming inside between her blinds. She took a quick peek to see if Red, her cardinal friend, was anywhere in sight. She glanced around and saw several birds flying in the clear sky above. Suddenly, Red appeared and landed on a branch quite close to her window. She gave him a smile and spoke softly. She knew better than to tap on the glass because she knew that would scare him away.

"How are you, my fine fellow? You don't know how lucky you are. You get to go wherever you like. I'm stuck indoors. I wish I could fly around out there with you."

The bird seemed to give Essie a little nod of its bright red head then flew away.

"Take care, Red," she called after him. When Joey arrived, Essie was still standing at the window looking morose.

"Miss Essie," he said. "What's wrong?"

"Good morning, Joey," she replied. "Just having a chat with Red, my friendly cardinal. I'm jealous of him because he can go flying around wherever he wants. No pandemic to tie him to one boring room."

"Maybe Red has his freedom," said Joey, "but he also doesn't get waffles for breakfast."

"Waffles?" she said, grabbing her walker and heading back to her recliner.

"That seemed to perk you up."

"Oh, Joey," she said. "I'm so disheartened that I can't find Carolyn. I'm not sure even waffles could make me feel better, although it has been quite a while since we've had them for breakfast."

"And they smell great too. I'm sure you'll track this Carolyn down, Miss Essie," he said as he placed the thermometer in her mouth.

"Ummmm—" she mumbled. Joey brought her breakfast over to her footstool and set it down. He took out the thermometer.

"Miss Essie, you're below normal," he said. "That usually isn't much to worry about, but I don't like seeing you so despondent."

"It's okay, Joey. I just didn't sleep very well. I couldn't stop thinking about why we can't find Carolyn."

"I'm sure you will. Just be patient, I mean, it's only been a few days."

"Yes, but when we met Carolyn she was in trouble. She was extremely upset. I'm not sure she has the time to wait for us to be patient. We need to find her now."

"Just keep working at it, Miss Essie. I'm sure you will. You're all working so hard."

Essie continued to look glum. Then, she realized that she had two duties and she was only focusing on one—finding Carolyn. She also needed to find out more information about Joey for their funding campaign, and here he was right in front of her and she was ignoring this opportunity.

"Please eat something, Miss Essie."

"Hmm, okay." She picked at the food and sighed. "What did you do yesterday evening, Joey?"

"Oh, just the regular," he replied. "Delivered food to customers, then went home and watched TV. Talked to a friend of mine out in California where I used to work."

"You used to work in California?"

"Yup," he said. "In Silicon Valley. Have you ever heard of that?"

"It's that big technical place, right?" she said.

"It's definitely that," he smiled.

"Did you like working there?" she asked as she slowly stuffed bites of waffle into her mouth.

"Well, I liked some of my co-workers, like the guy I was talking to last night," he responded, "but to tell the truth, Miss Essie, the place and the job really just weren't for me. When my parents needed me to help out with the restaurant, they didn't need to ask twice before I came right back home. I love this place, this town."

"That's good to hear. How long have you been back now?" she asked, hoping she wasn't sounding like she was prodding.

"Only a few months. When it became obvious that the pandemic was going to have this devastating, long-lasting effect on my parents' livelihood, I just really didn't have a choice. I wanted to be here for them. I mean, they've bent over backwards to give me so much."

"Do you have brothers and sisters?"

"Two younger sisters, so they're not a huge help although they both pitch in."

"I know that small businesses like your parents have can get loans from the government," she suggested.

"Oh, they have that, but it's just not enough. And it's not just their business; they're also worried about their workers who they had to lay off. Most of them haven't been able to find other work. My parents feel so guilty about them."

"Oh, no," said Essie. "This is all just so horrible. I wish there was something I could do."

"Well, maybe some night you might order a pizza, Miss

Essie."

"I had never thought about that," she said. "Is it hard? I've never ordered food. I don't even know if Happy Haven will allow residents to order in food from the outside, but I can't see any reason why they wouldn't."

"I don't know either. Let me check with some of the other aides. I've never delivered pizza here, but that doesn't mean that some resident here hasn't ordered takeout."

"And I'll ask Connie at the front desk. If any resident orders food brought in, she would know."

"That sounds great, Thanks, Miss Essie."

"I guess I'm done, Joey," Essie said, slurping up the last of her syrup-covered waffle. "You can take my tray with you."

"Great, Miss Essie. That saves a lot of time." He headed out.

After Joey had departed, Essie did as she had promised, and called the front desk to speak with Connie the receptionist.

"Hello, Connie, this is Essie Cobb."

"Good morning, Miss Essie. How can I help you?"

"Do any residents ever order food to be delivered?"

"Oh, that's a good question," said Connie. "I can't say that I know the answer. If they did order food, they could just call it in from their own phone. Of course, the delivery person would bring it here to the front desk. We get lots of deliveries but mostly flowers or packages. I'm trying to think if or when we ever had food delivered. I just can't remember."

"Is it forbidden?"

"Oh, no," said Connie. "It's just, I guess, most residents eat in the dining room—or rather—ate in the dining room before the pandemic so no one really needed food to be brought in. Why, Miss Essie? Are you bored with the chef's creations?"

"No, nothing like that, I was just curious."

"Well, sorry I couldn't be more help."

"Actually, Connie, you were a great help. Thank you."

After she'd finished talking to Connie, Essie realized that she needed to re-phone the numbers on her list of possible Carolyn Harpers in Bancroft Falls. She picked up the list and perused it. About half of the names on the list she had eliminated and crossed out from her previous day of phoning. The remaining names had question marks which was Essie's code meaning that there had been no answer, or an answering machine, or some other indication that she should phone again.

She began. With the first call, she got no answer at all, just continuous ringing. The person wasn't home and either didn't have an answering machine or hadn't turned it on. With the second call, she found the person home but her questions revealed quite quickly that no one named Carolyn Harper lived there or that anyone in the house knew her.

The third call led to an answering machine and she heard a recorded message of a woman saying that no one was home and to leave a message and she would get back to them. Essie left the same message that she'd left the first time she'd called with an extra exhortation of how important it was that the person return the call. She continued on in the same manner, until she had gone through most of the names that she hadn't been able to contact before.

Essie sat back in her chair, totally frustrated. Maybe Opal or Marjorie had had better luck. And yet, even as she sat there, that same strange feeling she'd had the previous day when she'd made the phone calls struck her again. She couldn't put her finger on it, but something about the calls or calling was bothering her. She thought and thought and couldn't figure it out.

Her reverie was interrupted by Joey bringing lunch.

"Oh no," she cried. "It can't be lunch time. I must have spent the entire morning on the phone."

"Did you find your Miss Carolyn?" asked Joey.

"No, deejay's PJs," said Essie. "Oh, sorry, Joey."

"That's fine, Miss Essie," Joey replied, chuckling. "I understand your frustration. I'm sure you'll find her soon—or maybe Miss Opal or Miss Marjorie will. I know you're all calling."

"We are. And Fay is trying to find her using her computer search tools."

"You ladies are a force to be reckoned with," he said. "And I asked around downstairs and no one seemed to know about food delivery for residents here. It doesn't seem to be forbidden in any way. I guess just nobody does it because everyone likes the food here."

"That's what I discovered too. Carolyn at the front desk said she couldn't remember any food deliveries, but we get flower deliveries and other packages all the time."

"Sounds like it's not forbidden," he said.

"Well, then, Joey, I see a pizza in my future. Can I just call Rizzolli's?"

"Here," he said, reaching into his pocket from under his plastic paraphernalia, "This is our business card. It has our phone number and a short list of our pizzas on it."

"Thanks. I'll keep it here on my table so I can order a pizza right away."

"Wonderful. I hope you enjoy it. Are you ladies Zooming again today?" he asked.

"Yes, we are. I think it's sort of become a standing date, as they say now."

"Good. I have my fingers crossed that you'll track down your Carolyn."

"Thanks," she said and waved at him as he headed out her door.

"Hmm," she said to herself. "How to order a pizza."

She lifted her received and called her daughter.

"Prudence."

"Hello, Mom. It's nice to hear from you. I'm getting ready to go to the grocery. Do you need me to pick up anything for you?"

"No. But I want to order a pizza."

"Oh, a pizza? Isn't that a bit spicy for you?"

"No, not a bit."

"Well, I can get you a small one at the grocery and bring it to you."

"No. That's not what I want. I want to order a pizza from Rizzoli's and have it delivered later today."

"Why?"

"That's my business."

"What are you up to, Mom?"

"Is ordering food for delivery being 'up to something'?"

"No, but, well, I guess you can call them and place an order and have them deliver it to you, but truly it would be just as easy for me to get you one and bring it to you. It's on my way and…"

"No. I want a delivery pizza from Rizzoli's this afternoon." demanded Essie. Then she sighed. "I'm sorry, dear, I don't mean to sound like a gruff old buffalo but I really want to do this."

"Okay, Mom," replied Prudence. "Oh, there is a problem."

"What?"

"How are you going to pay for a delivery pizza?"

"I have my own checking account."

"Yes, but Mom, for a delivery pizza, and—particularly now

with this pandemic—you can't write a check for a pizza. You're going to have to use a credit card and you don't have a credit card…"

"Well, I just never needed one, since you pay all my bills from my account. I really don't even need the bank account."

"All right, Mom, here's what I'll do. You tell me what kind of pizza you want and I'll call Rizzoli's and order it on my credit card and have them deliver it to you…"

"Well, dear, that sounds as if it would work technically, but you see, I was planning on ordering four pizzas and having them sent to my friends during our Zoom meeting so we could all eat pizza while we Zoom."

"While you Zoom?" cried Pru, aghast. "Mom, what are you up to over there? Please tell me, you're not getting into more trouble."

"Of course not," said Essie. "How about you order four small cheese pizzas from Rizolli's and put them on your credit card and then write a check to yourself from my account?"

"Oh, I suppose," said Pru. "Who should they deliver them to?"

Essie gave her daughter her friends' names and room numbers and asked that they deliver the pizzas around three o'clock. Prudence promised to fulfill her end of the bargain and the two women concluded their phone call.

Chapter 15

Essie was excited about the afternoon Zoom meeting. She had finished her repeat calls to the unresponsive Harper numbers in Bancroft Falls after lunch but hadn't had any greater success than she'd had in the morning. Pru had called her back to tell her that she'd ordered small cheese pizzas to be delivered around three to all four of the lady friends in time for the Zoom meeting.

"Oh, aardvark yardmark," said Essie out loud. "This will be like a party."

She fluffed her hair and even put on a new, clean shirt. With a freshly powdered nose, she was ready to Zoom.

Shortly before three, there was a knock on her door. When she opened it, one of the staff members—complete with face mask and gloves—was standing there with a small square box. The aroma that wafted from it was amazing.

"Delivery for you, Miss Essie," said the young woman.

"Thank you," said Essie, taking the pizza from her and returning inside her apartment.

She took the box to her kitchen and unpacked it. The pizza inside looked delicious—all bubbly and rich. She picked up one slice, slid it onto a dessert plate from her cupboard and placed it on her walker. Then she scooted quickly over to her sofa and sat in front of her computer. She had it plugged in and turned on, already set to the Zoom location.

She checked her watch. It was exactly three. She pressed her host button and her camera light popped on and her image appeared in the little box.

"Hello," she said. "It's Zoom time. Is anyone there?"

"Hi, Grandma," said Ned, his picture box appearing on the screen. "Where are your lady friends?"

"Oh, they should be here any minute, Ned. I sent them all a little surprise so that might be taking some time." She smiled at Ned. "Sorry I couldn't send the surprise to you, Ned, but…"

"Essie," cried Opal, her screen image showing up with Opal holding a slice of pizza in her hand. "Did you send me this pizza?"

"I did, Opal. It's from Joey's family restaurant."

"How lovely," said Opal, "and how delicious. It's nothing like the pizza we get every so often in the dining room. It's much cheesier and spicier."

"Essie." Marjorie popped on the screen as did Fay. Both ladies had pizza in their hands and—in Fay's case—in her mouth.

"This is fabulous," said Ned. "Everyone just remain exactly like you are. I need to take a screen shot. Everyone! Bite on that pizza and smile." All the ladies did as directed; it wasn't a difficult demand. "Great. That'll make a super addition to our funding website for Joey's family restaurant."

"When do you think you'll have it ready, Ned?" asked Essie.

"Probably tomorrow," said Ned. "Some last minute touch up,

and filing all the info with the website so that Joey's family will get any money raised."

"Speaking of money," said Opal, "I was able to speak with several bankers I know from my previous job and I asked about the Rizzoli family—or rather the Rizzoli restaurant. Of course, none of them could tell me anything official but one fellow had worked with the family on funding when they'd extended their building and had applied for a loan. He said that the family was extremely responsible, always repaid loans on time. He said like most small family restaurants, they were suffering terribly during the pandemic and he said the odds were probably fifty-fifty as to whether they could survive. I asked him about a funding campaign and whether it would help, and he said that if any group would do that for the family, it might help them get through the worst of the pandemic. He said government grants were just stop-gap measures."

"I'm so glad to hear that," said Ned, "because we're almost ready to go with our fund drive. And as for ordering pizza from Rizzoli's, I suggest you all contact everyone you know there at Happy Haven and encourage them to order pizza delivered regularly. After all, it's for one of their own."

"We'll do that, Ned," said Essie. All three women nodded.

"Okay," said Ned, "now that we have that covered, let's discuss the issue of Carolyn Harper. What do any of you have to report?"

"I went through my list again," said Marjorie, but I didn't find any new information."

"Same here," said Opal.

"Ned," said Essie. "My list didn't reveal anything new either, but I might have one small new piece of information from the call I made to the senior center."

"Why don't you tell us," said Ned.

"Okay," said Essie. "This time when I called, I got a gentleman named Phil and I started out by confessing that I'd called the previous time and lied…"

"Oh, Essie, was that wise?" asked Opal.

'Well, I don't know," replied Essie, "but I believe that my honesty worked to some extent anyway. I explained to Phil how extremely concerned we all are about Carolyn. I told him what we've determined from our investigation so far. I said we believed she lived in Bancroft Falls and that she had visited the Senior Center the other day and accidentally signed into our Zoom meeting. I explained that we were worried that she was trying to find Will and was unable to locate him and that we all felt responsible and wanted to help her. Phil was very polite and after I told him what we'd discovered on our own, he had me talk to a lady named Gloria who's the receptionist there. She sits at the main desk and can see out the front window, as she said. She can see when clients arrive—whether by car or if they walk up. She remembered Carolyn. She said she saw her arrive on foot from the north."

"Is that important?" asked Marjorie.

"As it turns out, yes," said Essie. "If she'd come from the south, Gloria said, she might have gotten off at the bus stop which is south of the Center. Gloria said that the fact that she arrived on foot from the north means that she must have walked there from a residential area."

"Yes," said Ned. "That's exactly what I was thinking. Fay, do you still have that downtown map of Bancroft Falls that shows the location of the senior center?"

With that, Fay pressed a button on her end, or whatever she had to do, and all of a sudden, the map of Bancroft Falls filled everyone's screen.

"Okay," said Ned. "Can you all see the senior center?" He

used a digital pointer to show the center, moving the map around until the center was located on the bottom of the screen. "I'm going to put it here so we can see many of the residential streets north of the center. Can you all read the street names on your screen?"

"Can you make it little larger, Fay?" asked Opal. Fay obliged and the screen map increased in size.

"That's good. I can read the street names now," said Opal.

"Me too," said Essie.

"Ladies, this is what I want you to do now. One at a time, go through those lists and give each address you have listed for a potential Carolyn to Fay. Just the address for the people you haven't yet contacted or those you're not sure about. About how many are we talking about?" asked Ned.

"I have two or three," said Essie, counting up her list.

"Me too," said Opal.

"About that for me too, I think," answered Marjorie.

"Okay," said Ned, "Fay, as they read out these addresses, can you put an X in about the location where you think it would go on the street on the map? If you can't find the street, we'll put that on hold for a while because it probably means it's too far away for someone to walk to the Center. Okay, Grandma, let's start with your addresses."

"Fine," said Essie. "How are we going to mark these to know who's in which house?"

"Fay, why don't you just put the first name of the Harper in the nearest location you can find? None of this is perfect. We just want to get an idea of what we have and possibly, how many of those Harpers might live in the right vicinity."

Fay gave a thumbs up in her small window at the very top of the screen. It was clear she knew what she was doing.

"Well," Essie began, "the first name that I could not locate and the address that goes with it is Carl Harper at 1203 Rose Street."

They all watched as Fay's head bent down. They could see the shadow of her hand fly over the screen. When Fay lifted her hand, everyone could see where she had placed an X and written "Carl" on a side street a few blocks north of the senior center.

Essie read out her remaining unknown Harpers and Fay added those to the map as well. Then it was Opal's turn. Opal provided her names and addresses and Fay quickly located those Harpers on the map. After Marjorie added her two Harpers and Fay had placed them with X's and first names, the four women and Ned just stared at the little street map of the downtown and surrounding area of the Bancroft Falls Senior Citizens' Services Center. Little X's with names appeared all over the map.

"Well, ladies," said Ned. "This is probably the best clue we have so far. I feel sure that one of these X's represents our Carolyn Harper. Now the question is, how to determine which X she is and how to contact her. It seems she won't or can't answer her landline phone."

"That is the question," said Marjorie.

"Could we hire somebody to just go door to door there and knock and ask at these houses if Carolyn is there?" asked Essie.

"Who would that someone be?" asked Opal. "I don't know anyone there, do you?"

"Well, we now know several people at the Senior Citizens' Services Center," said Essie.

"Essie," said Marjorie, "don't you think we've imposed on them enough?"

"Hey," said Ned. "Now, let's don't fight. Let's use our brain power."

"If Marjorie has any," scowled Opal.

"Look who's talking," retorted Marjorie.

"Pizza!" cried out Essie.

"I know, Essie," said Opal, "It was delicious. Thank you."

"No, I mean, pizza delivery in Bancroft Falls."

"That doesn't make any sense," said Opal.

"Wait a minute," said Ned. "I think I see what Grandma may be getting at."

"And what is that?" asked Marjorie.

"Tell us your idea, Grandma," said Ned, grinning.

"Well," said Essie, "I was thinking we could find a pizza restaurant there in Bancroft Falls and order pizza to be delivered to all of our unknown addresses. Maybe we could tell them we'd pay them even if the person wasn't home but that we wanted them to report to us who accepted the pizza and who didn't."

"What good would that do?" asked Opal.

"I'm thinking that if we delivered a pizza to a Carolyn Harper at each of our unknown addresses we could learn something, particularly if the pizza restaurant was willing to report back to us whether or not they could deliver the pizza."

"I think it's a very clever idea," said Ned. "It's actually sort of like hiring a detective to go and investigate all of our unknown addresses, but probably at a much lower cost. It will probably turn out that this method will allow us to eliminate even more addresses and then maybe we'll want to consider hiring an actual private detective."

"Mott's pots!" cried Essie. "I love the idea of hiring a private detective."

"You would, Essie," said Opal. "Everything is a crime spree to you."

"No, Opal," said Essie, "Everything is a mystery to me."

"All right," said Ned. "Let's not jump the gun. I've marked down the addresses. Fay, can you check there in Bancroft Falls to see if…"

Before Ned could finish his sentence, Fay had a poster on the screen for three pizza parlors in Bancroft Falls.

"Wonderful," cried Ned. "I think I'll pick Nero's Pizza as it appears to be just a block north of the Senior Center so they'll probably deliver to everyone in our designated area. I'll just jot down their number. Ladies, let me take care of this order. I have the original list of Harpers and I've marked down all of these changes so I know which ones to send the pizzas to…"

"That would be good, Ned, because Pru had to order the pizza we have here,"

"Oh, Essie, doesn't your daughter trust you with a credit card?" teased Marjorie.

"She trusts me; I just don't have time for it." Essie knew this was a fib but she was embarrassed to admit that she didn't want a credit card because she considered it a hassle.

"Anyway," said Ned, trying to prevent another tiff among the elderly women on the Zoom chat, "I've jotted down the number for Nero's Pizza. I'm going to call as soon as we end our Zoom call. I hope they'll go along with our plan and that I hear back from them tonight some time. I'll report on the results tomorrow at our three o'clock meeting and also I should be able to show you our webpage for Joey's 'fund me' site then too."

So, Ned," said Essie, "what should we do in the meantime?"

"I would keep calling those numbers in Bancroft Falls. Maybe try calling at a different time of day? Maybe the person works. Maybe they're so busy they don't check their answering machine very often. Anyway, we have a handful of potential Carolyn Harpers still out there—all very viable. I'll use the pizza ploy, but you ladies keep at it through the front door, so to speak."

"We will, Ned," said Essie. The other three ladies nodded and gladly agreed to do their part.

Chapter 16

Later, sometime after the meeting, Ned called Essie back.

"Grandma, hi. I ordered the pizza from Nero's sent to all of the names and addresses we marked as possibilities. I asked if they would let me put a note inside the pizzas but they said they couldn't really do that. They did say that if I paid by my credit card—which I did—that that information would go on the receipt attached to the box and the person getting the pizza could easily see who it came from. It wouldn't include my full credit card number, for obvious reasons, but it would have my name and my phone number. I'm hoping that at least some of the people will be grateful for the pizza—or at least curious— and will try to contact me. If that happens, I'm only going to give them a brief explanation. I will try to get them to contact you for the full story."

"Me?" Essie asked.

"Yes, you're the one who's more or less coordinating the interactions with people about the identity of Carolyn. I think it best that you speak directly to any of these people who might call me. I just wanted to let you know so that you won't be surprised if you get any calls."

"I'm glad you gave me a warning, Ned. It would be strange to hear from some unknown person about this out of the blue."

"Well, you have been leaving voice mail on lots of answering machines so it wouldn't be completely out of the blue. Anyway, let's hope we get something. Maybe not the actual identity of Carolyn and the nature of her plight, but perhaps we might be able to eliminate some of the folks who are on the list of possibles."

"Yes, let's hope," said Essie.

After she finished speaking with Ned, she got ready for bed. All that really meant was that she changed out of her loose sweat pants into her loose pajama pants and changed out of her loose sweat shirt into her loose pajama top. She brushed her teeth and used the toilet. Then she wheeled herself into her bedroom. She had barely sat down on her bed when her phone rang.

"My goodness, this is late," she said aloud, glancing at her alarm clock on her nightstand. It said nine p.m. She scooted over and grabbed the receiver from the telephone next to her bed.

"Hello," she said.

"Is this Essie Cobb?" said a male voice.

"Yes," she replied.

"My name is Lionel Harper," he said. "I just spoke with your grandson and he said I should call you to thank you for the pizza. My wife and I received it and really enjoyed it; it's been ages since we've had a pizza. I've forgotten how good they are. What a lovely treat when we're so depressed from being stuck at home all day during this awful pandemic."

"Thank you, Mr. Harper," Essie replied. "Actually, there was a reason we sent pizza to you. We actually sent pizzas to a number of people named Harper who live in Bancroft Falls."

"Really?" he asked. "Why is that? Is this some sort of trick for one of those reality shows?"

"Oh, no," said Essie. "We're trying to track down a lady who lives in your town named Carolyn Harper. I won't go into the whys and wherefores but it's actually rather important that we get in touch with her. Unfortunately, we don't know her address or phone number; only that she lives in Bancroft Falls. And we know she's in some sort of trouble, or at least someone she knows named Will is in trouble, or possibly sick. You wouldn't by any chance know Carolyn, would you?"

"No," he said. "I don't know anyone besides us named Harper here in Bancroft Falls."

"That's odd because there are quite a number of Harpers there."

"Really? Well, what do you know? I guess I don't get out much. Certainly not with this pandemic."

"And you and your wife don't have any relatives named Carolyn or know any other Harpers in Bancroft Falls?"

"No, as I said, I thought we were the only ones."

"Well, Mr. Harper, I guarantee you're not, but if you don't know Carolyn or any Harpers in your town, I guess there's nothing else I can ask you."

"Well, I'm sorry I couldn't help you, Mrs. Cobb," he replied.

"Oh, you did help. Every Harper in Bancroft Falls I can contact is one more I can cross off my list. If I can eliminate all except one, that person should be the Harper I'm looking for."

"I don't mean to be presumptuous, but have you thought of going to the police? You said it was a serious issue."

"Yes, it does seem to be so to Carolyn, but I'm not certain that it would necessarily be considered as such by the police, and until I can be certain that there is some crime, or life or death issue at play, I think it best that we search for her on our own. But I thank you so much for calling. And I'm glad you enjoyed the pizza."

"Thank you again. If I hear anything about Carolyn, I will call you back," he said and the call ended.

Essie crawled into bed and under her covers. She was certainly tired, but she just couldn't get to sleep. She was wondering if Lionel Harper was right. Maybe they should contact the police in Bancroft Falls. The police could always tell her to go away, that her worries were nothing, that Carolyn Harper was fine. But how would they know that unless they checked on her? Essie thought that maybe she might be able to at least get the local police in Bancroft Falls to check up on Carolyn, just to be certain she was okay. But what to say? How to approach them? Should she call or have Ned call? She just didn't know what to do or say? And these thoughts ran through her mind most of the night.

When morning finally arrived, Essie was anything but well-rested. She looked at her alarm clock and couldn't believe it was time to get up. Even though she was incredibly exhausted, she rolled herself out of her bed and got ready as quickly as possible. She was determined to do something—she wasn't certain at this point what that something was—but she knew in her heart that she couldn't just wait and do nothing. She felt that Carolyn needed her help and she needed it now. In fact, Essie reasoned, it might already be too late. That thought simply petrified her.

She checked out her window, but Red didn't seem to be around this morning. Maybe he'd flown to New York State to look for Carolyn Harper? She wished she could do that. Lucky cardinals.

When Joey arrived with her breakfast, she decided to ask him what he thought she should do.

"What's this on your counter, Miss Essie?" he asked, pointing to the Rizzoli pizza box with a few slices left inside.

"Joey, we did as you suggested and ordered pizza from your restaurant. It was fabulous. I had it delivered to all my friends to eat during our Zoom meeting yesterday. They loved it too."

"Oh, I guess my Dad must have brought it then. He does the delivery until I get there. We usually don't get many orders before three."

"Probably so. I'm going to tell everyone to order pizza from your restaurant. It's so much better than the pizza they make in the dining room."

"And you're saving these slices for lunch?"

"Yes. You can skip my tray today at noon if you want," she said.

"Okay, Miss Essie."

She stirred her dry cereal with her spoon while Joey took her temperature. She was planning what to ask him.

"Ninety-eight point four," he said. "Nice and normal."

"Good," replied Essie, still twirling her spoon in her cereal as Joey returned the thermometer back into its case and placed it back in his side carrier that he wore over his shoulder.

"Joey," she said, "what do you think I should do about Carolyn?"

"Oh," he replied, "I don't know. What have you done so far?"

"Well, we've tried to find her," she replied, still twirling the spoon. "We've called every Harper in Bancroft Falls within walking distance of the senior center. I've spoken to several workers at the center trying to get them to tell me anything they remember about her from the day she came in and used their computer."

"That all sounds good," he said. "Are you sure she lives within walking distance of the center?"

"Well, fairly sure," said Essie. "We know from Gloria, the receptionist that Carolyn must have walked to the center as she arrived from the north, so that would mean she came from a home and not the bus stop which is on the south side of the center. Gloria remembers seeing her arrive."

"That's good information," said Joey. "How are you sure you have all the Harpers in Bancroft Falls?"

"We're not," she replied. "But we know Carolyn is an older lady so we're assuming she has a landline phone."

"That might be a big assumption," he said. "Most people these days have cell phones and those phones aren't listed in phone directories."

"I know," said Essie, "but we're counting on Carolyn being of an age where she would still have a landline too and would be listed, even if she isn't listed under her first name."

"I see what you mean," he said. "Even so, those are a lot of assumptions."

"I know," she replied, "but how can we get a list of all the Carolyn Harpers in Bancroft Falls with cell phones?"

"Good question," said her aide. "Miss Essie, are you going to eat that cereal or play with it?" He looked sternly at her from out of his plastic face mask.

"Oh, Joey, I can't stomach anything right now. Just take it away."

With a glum expression, Joey picked up the tray and silently left Essie's apartment. *It's true. Joey's right*, she thought. It was quite possible that their Carolyn Harper didn't even have a landline telephone and wasn't listed in the Bancroft Falls directory. Like so many people these days—not Essie, of course—Carolyn probably had a cell phone. Essie picked up her list of landline phone numbers for people named Harper in Bancroft Falls. Only two Harpers remained unexplained on her list. Every time she looked at this list, Essie realized, she got a strange feeling. What was it? She looked at the two numbers that remained a mystery to her. With a sigh, she phoned the first one again—a Carl Harper. Each time she'd called this number she'd gotten the same answering machine message and—sure, enough—here it was again.

"No one can come to the phone right now. Please leave a message and someone will return your call," said the woman. *Hmm,* thought Essie. She wondered about the message. She'd heard it now several times. One thing strange about it that was unlike some of the other messages was that it didn't mention the Harpers' name. The woman didn't say that Carl Harper or his wife, if this was indeed his wife's voice, wasn't—"

"Oh, Lordy Mordy!" cried Essie so loudly that she had to look at her front door to be sure no one would come running in to check on her. "I know why I've been so concerned about these names. It's this name—Carl Harper. It's this voice message. Not just any voice message—and not just any voice. This is the voice of our Carolyn." *Oh, my*, she thought. *What should I do? Should I call Opal or Marjorie? Or Ned? No. Just a minute.* As the voice on the answering machine continued to speak and direct the listener to leave a message, Essie decided to again do just that.

She pressed the message button and spoke into the receiver. "Carolyn!" she cried out for the message machine. "Carolyn Harper. I know this is you. This is Essie Cobb. You don't know me, but I know you. You happened upon our Zoom meeting the other day when you were at the Bancroft Falls Senior Citizens' Service Center, and since then my friends and I have been so worried about you. I recognize your voice. Please pick up." She waited. No response. "Carolyn, if you're not there, when you get this, please call me back. We want to help you." Essie left her phone number and hung up. Then she sat there staring at her phone, practically willing it to ring. "Come on, Carolyn. If you're there, please call me. I won't hurt you. I want to help you."

For the next several hours, Essie sat riveted to her chair. She was so certain that Carolyn would return her call. She didn't even want to go to her bathroom for fear of missing a call from the missing woman. However, no one called and around lunch time, Joey arrived with her meal tray.

"Miss Essie, I know you said you didn't want lunch, and I know you have that leftover pizza, but I thought I'd bring you a tray anyway in case you changed your mind."

"Oh, Joey," said Essie. "It's you." Her disheartened face continued to stare at the phone.

"I'm sorry, Miss Essie," said the young man, as he placed her lunch before her. "Expecting a call from your new beau?"

"No, of course not," She responded. "I'm expecting a call from Carolyn."

"You found your missing lady?" he asked.

"I did. I tracked her down. I know who she is. I know what her number is. I know her address. I even left her a voice mail and told her to contact me. I just can't figure out why she hasn't responded."

"Well, maybe she's out of town or at the store," said Joey.

"I hope it's something simple like that and that nothing horrible has happened to her," replied Essie.

"Do you think it's possible that something bad has happened?" he asked.

"I don't know," said Essie. "All we know is that she was

terribly distraught when she spoke to us on Zoom. If I could just get her to contact me, then I'd know for sure if it was something serious or something frivolous."

"You know, even if it's frivolous, Miss Essie, you could still call the police. Just the fact that you're all so worried about this lady makes it seem to me that a call to them is warranted."

"I know. I know. But I think I'll just give it a little longer and hope she'll contact me."

"Okay, Miss Essie," said Joey. "You're the boss."

"Oh, Joey," said Essie, with a smile. "I am definitely not the boss—and I never have been."

"I would love you for my boss, Miss Essie," said Joey, and out he went.

Chapter 17

Essie waited all afternoon, and Carolyn never returned her call. She realized almost too late that it was nearly time for their Zoom meeting. She was excited to tell her friends that she had found Carolyn, and anxious to ask them all what to do next.

At three o'clock, Essie had fixed herself up and was sitting on her sofa in front of her laptop computer with her camera and audio all ready. At exactly three p.m., she pressed the blue Zoom button to start the meeting, and Fay and Opal appeared on the screen.

"Good afternoon, ladies," said Essie. Opal replied and Fay waved. Marjorie appeared and greeted the threesome. Then, almost as quickly, Ned arrived and greetings were made all around.

"May I start?" asked Essie. "I have amazing news." Everyone was excited. "I found Carolyn," she announced.

"What?" said Opal. "Where is she? In Bancroft Falls?"

"Yes, she's there," said Essie.

"Is she on the list?" asked Marjorie. "Did she walk to the

Center? Why did she barge into our Zoom session?"

"Who is Will?" asked Opal, "and why is she so worried about him?"

"Wait a minute," said Essie. "I found her, but I haven't spoken to her."

"If you haven't spoken to her, how do you know you found her?" asked Marjorie.

"I was calling the numbers on the list again, and I realized that the woman's voice on the answering machine for Carl Harper was Carolyn's. I know her voice. So I left her a message and explained everything we've been doing since she barged into our Zoom meeting and that we only want to help her. Now I'm just waiting for her to call back."

"Grandma," said Ned, "when did you leave this message?"

"This morning when I realized it was her. I've been sitting here waiting for her to call back. I'm sure she will now that she knows we're worried about her and all that we've been doing to help her."

"Hmm," said Ned. "I'm not so sure. We don't know what's going on with Carolyn. We don't know what has happened to upset her, and we don't know if she wants to return your call or even if she *can* return it…"

"Right, Essie," agreed Opal. "Remember, she's trying to find Will. Maybe she thinks you've taken Will, and now you've scared her even more."

"Why would she think that, Opal?" said Essie. "Why would four old ladies on Zoom have her husband? Or son?"

"I don't know, Essie," said Marjorie. "Just because we're old doesn't mean we aren't capable of enticing a nice-looking gentleman away from his spouse…"

"Marjorie," cried Essie. "I'm sure she doesn't think that about us."

"All right. All right," said Ned. "This isn't getting us anywhere. Ladies, let's stop and think for a minute. Just because Grandma left this message on Carl Harper's answering machine does not necessarily mean we have found our Carolyn…"

"Yes it does," said Essie. "I tell you, I recognize her voice from the Zoom meeting."

"Okay, Grandma, but just to be sure, let me check something out first."

"What?" asked Essie.

"Well, one simple thing. I'm going to call Carl Harper's phone and record the message left by the supposed Carolyn. Then I'm going to compare the audio of her voice on that recording with the voice of the lady who appeared on our Zoom meeting. I've saved a screen recording of that meeting—— actually I've saved all of our Zoom meetings. There are a number of digital audio programs available that can pretty much verify whether or not the two voices are the same."

"You can do that, Ned?"

"Yes, it's quite easy. I'll have a fairly large sample from both recordings——I only need a word or two to do the analysis. I'll do that after our meeting today and let Grandma know as soon as I do, and she can call you all and let you know. There's no reason to pursue this Carl Harper phone number and address if we're not positive we're dealing with the actual woman who came into our meeting."

"That's the kipper's nippers," said Essie, and the three other ladies on the screen nodded or motioned their delight.

"So, let's put that concern aside for now," said Ned. "What I wanted to show you all today is what I've been working on." He pushed a button and everyone's box disappeared as a website appeared on the screen. Ned's voice continued, "This is Joey's page on Save-Me.com." Across the screen the ladies could see a beautiful array of photographs all centered around a headshot of Joey without his pandemic paraphernalia. He was——as Marjorie had stated earlier——a very handsome young man. Placed around him were images of his family, including his parents, their restaurant, and their customers. Down in one corner were photos of Joey doing work at Happy Haven, including the shot that Ned had taken the other day of all of them eating pizza. Ned had somehow morphed the photo so it looked as if all four ladies were gathered around Joey in his strange gear.

"Oh, my, Ned," declared Essie. "It looks as if we were all here together with Joey."

"And we weren't," added Opal.

"The wonders of digital photography," said Ned modestly. "And look down at the bottom. That's where it tells the story of how dire the restaurant's plight is. Then right below that is the link people can click to donate money to the 'Joey Rizzoli Save Me Campaign.'"

"I wonder if anyone will donate money," said Essie.

"What's that below?" asked Marjorie, pointing to a digital counter.

"That's an indicator of the amount of money that has been donated so far. Right now, it stands at $655.23."

"Mothers' druthers," said Essie. "How long have you had this in progress?"

"It's been online only since this morning——so four or five hours."

"I can't believe that people from all over who don't even know Joey are donating money to help him and his family's restaurant," said Opal.

"People are really generous," said Essie.

"It's amazing," agreed Marjorie.

"Ned," said Essie, "how long will this last? How do we get the money to Joey?"

"Don't worry, Grandma," said Ned. "This platform is well established. We can let it run as long as necessary. I've run other campaigns through it."

"You have?" she asked.

"Yes, for some charities at work," he said. "It's very safe. You see right there in that box is where people enter their name and credit card number, and that box is where they indicate the amount of money they want to donate."

"And Joey and his parents don't know anything about this?" asked Opal.

"Well, they're probably going to find out now that it's online. Someone is bound to tell them, but I would suggest that none of you tell him. Just let it be a big surprise, okay?"

They all agreed to keep the surprise from Joey as long as possible.

There was some more general discussion, but the group disbanded agreeing to continue looking for Carolyn and to meet again the next day at the same time.

Essie watched television for the rest of the afternoon. She couldn't concentrate on any of the shows——even *Wheel of Fortune*, her favorite show——because all she could think about was Carolyn and where she might be and if she was okay.

Shortly before dinner, she got a telephone call.

"Hi, Grandma," said Ned. "Thought you'd like to be the first to know. You were right."

"Well, that's nothing new," said Essie, smiling.

"True," he replied. "You know your voices. The two voices are definitely the same. It was even obvious to me——and I'm no acoustics expert. But I had a friend of mine from work who does audio analysis check it out too and he said the voices on the two tapes are identical. Either that, or one of the women is a voice actress."

"I doubt that," said Essie.

"You really have a good ear, Grandma," he said. "You should be doing something with that amazing gift."

"And what would that be?"

"I don't know, maybe something in the record industry."

"Ha," she said. "Anyway, now that we know we've found our Carolyn, I guess it's okay for me to keep calling that number."

"I don't know," he replied. "The fact that she hasn't responded is not a good sign. I think it indicates that either she isn't there or she doesn't want anyone to know she's there."

"You really think so?" asked Essie.

"I do," said Ned. "I just don't see any reason why she would avoid contacting you when you obviously are trying to help her."

"If that's the case, then what do we do next?" she asked.

"I don't know yet, but I'm thinking about it. You should think about it too. I have great faith in your ideas, Grandma."

"Okay, Ned," said Essie. "I'll put on my thinking cap, and I won't make any more calls until our Zoom meeting tomorrow."

"Good girl," he replied.

They said good-bye and Essie got ready for dinner.

Chapter 18

After dinner, Essie watched some television. Claudia called and regaled her with tales of Ned's new baby. Claudia had talked to Shanna, and Shanna had sent her videos of the newborn and was still feeling sad beyond belief that Ned was off at a convention.

"But, dear," said Essie, "you get to see your first grandchild. Isn't that special?"

"Yes, Mom, it's wonderful. But I'm worried about Shanna. I'm afraid she might have those post-partum blues."

"Oh no," said Essie. "I hope not. Do you think you should let Ned know?"

"Shanna made me promise not to tell him how sad she is. I can see she's really trying, but I'm just sure she needs something more than extra help from her mother-in-law."

"Still, it's nice that you live out there so close to them," said Essie.

"It is. I love being a grandma. But what good does it do to be in such close proximity when this pandemic forces us to stay apart?"

"I'm sorry, dear. Just enjoy being a grandma, even if it is from afar. It truly is the best. All of the fun and none of the work," said Essie.

"I'm not sure I can agree with you, Mom. I feel like I've done more with this grandchild than any of my own children and all I can do is talk to Shanna on the phone. She's so tired all the time, I feel like I have to be there for her——and the baby."

"I'm sure she'll bounce right back as soon as Ned gets home."

"You're probably right. But I don't see any sign that his boss is going to let that happen any time soon."

"That's too bad. Ned is really an amazing young man. I'm sure if he could be back home with his little family, he could cheer that wife of his up in no time."

"I think you're right," said Claudia.

"He's been helping me and my friends solve a problem," said Essie.

"Your friends from your dinner table?" Claudia knew that Essie spent a lot of time with the ladies she ate with on a regular basis.

"Yes," said Essie. "He got us all Zooming."

"Oh my goodness, Mom. That's amazing. I bet you all love that."

"We do, but there are lots of strange things that go on in some of these Zoom meetings."

"Oh, I bet. Like your friend Marjorie is probably flirting with all the men on the screen, right?"

"Well, actually, it's just been the four of us——and one lady from upper New York State."

"What? Why would you have someone from New York on a Zoom chat?"

"Oh, nothing, dear," said Essie. "We get people from all over. You'd be surprised. Anyway, Ned helped us get it set up. He's really a remarkable young man."

"He is that," said Claudia. "I guess I'd better get going. I've got a husband to feed. Give my best to your friends."

"I will, dear."

Essie finished talking to her youngest daughter and went back to watching television. Later, she got ready for bed and was just crawling under the covers when the telephone on her nightstand rang.

"Hello," she said.

"I don't know why you're calling me," said an angry female voice that Essie immediately recognized as the mysterious Carolyn Harper. "Why are you doing this to me? Where is Will? Please bring him back. Please. I have what you want. I'm following your directions. Please." She screamed this last plea into the receiver then started to cry uncontrollably, and suddenly, she hung up.

Oh my, thought Essie. *How dreadful.* She thought about what to do. Should she immediately return the call? She knew Carolyn's number and obviously she was at home now. But she feared that given Carolyn's state of mind, another call from someone whom she obviously didn't trust would not be the best way to handle this volatile situation. She thought about calling Ned, but then remembered the call she'd just had with Claudia and decided she needed to let Ned alone for a while. What a dilemma.

"Oh, steady Freddy," said Essie, biting her lip and taking a deep breath. "Six of one, half a dozen of another." She grabbed her walker and headed out to the living room. Plopping herself into her recliner, she picked up her list of Harpers in Bancroft Falls, and quickly located the number for Carl Harper. Before she could change her mind, she called the number. It rang once.

"Hello," said a female voice that Essie knew was Carolyn's. There was an intensity that she could hear in the woman's tone. Then, just waiting and some very audible breathing.

"Carolyn?" said Essie. No answer. But she didn't hang up. "Carolyn, my name is Essie Cobb. I am one of the ladies on the Zoom call you were on the other day when you went to the senior citizens' center in Bancroft Falls."

"You told me to call that number," said Carolyn in an intense voice.

"No," said Essie. "My friends and I were having a meeting, and you just showed up. None of us knew who you were. We only became worried because of what you said about Will and searching for him, and him being missing. None of us had ever seen you before."

"Then how did I get to your site? I typed in the number you said to use."

"I don't know what you mean," said Essie. "I didn't give you the Zoom number as I've never met you before."

"You left it on my door."

"Your door?"

"Yes," said Carolyn. "You know you did. You put the directions in an envelope and taped it to my front door."

"I'm really confused, Carolyn," said Essie. "I don't know where you live, or at least I didn't then. I couldn't put anything on your door. I live hundreds of miles away from you in the Happy Haven Assisted Living Facility."

"This doesn't make sense," said Carolyn.

"That is surely true," said Essie. "Maybe we could start from the beginning and you could explain what happened, and maybe together we can figure things out——and what has happened to Will."

At Will's name, Carolyn burst into tears.

"Oh, Carolyn, I'm so sorry; I didn't mean to upset you."

"Never mind," she said. "I'll explain. I'm not sure I trust you, but right now I just don't know what else to do." She cried and then halted the tears. "It's just that either you have him...or someone else has him."

"Will?" asked Essie.

"Yes," she cried, gulping for air.

"Carolyn, if someone has taken him, that is kidnapping. You need to contact the police."

"No!" she screamed. "You, or...they said if I tell anyone they'll kill him."

"Oh dear," cried Essie. "I know you're scared, Carolyn. But that's kidnapping. You can't keep the police in the dark. This is a crime. You have to call the police."

"No!"

"Carolyn, please. If you want to see your husband again, you have to let the police know he's been kidnapped."

"My husband?"

"Yes. Will."

"My husband is Carl. Carl Harper. He died three years ago."

"Then is Will your...son?"

"No. Will is my dog," said Carolyn, breaking into a new round of tears.

"So, you're telling me that someone kidnapped your dog..."

"Yes, they just took him from the back-yard. I didn't know he was gone. He stays out there for hours some times. I only realized when I opened the front door and there was this envelope taped there. It said if I ever wanted to see my dog again, I would follow the directions. I had to go to the bank and withdraw ten thousand dollars all in hundred-dollar bills and put them in an envelope. I'm supposed to tape the envelope to our mailbox on the street in front of our house tomorrow night. They gave me a number that I could type into a computer so I could see a live feed of Will online to be sure he was okay, but I don't have a computer. I knew they had computers at the senior center, so I ran down there as fast as I could and got on the computer and typed in this code they gave me, but instead of seeing Will...."

"You saw me and my friends on Zoom."

"Right. I tried it again, but each time I got something different. I was never able to see a live feed of Will like they said I would. I'm so afraid they've already killed him. I'm afraid if I leave the money on the mailbox tomorrow night, I'll never get him back, but I'm also afraid that if I don't leave the money, they'll kill him. I don't know what to do."

"I don't know either, Carolyn, but one thing I do know. My friends and I are not a part of this horrible plot against your dog Will. We all love animals. We would never do anything like this. We are very concerned for you, and we all have worried about you since you popped into our Zoom meeting the other day. We have been doing everything we could think of to find you and help you. Believe me, it has been very hard to track you down."

"Oh my," said Carolyn, pausing as her breathing calmed. "I do believe you. I do. And for the first time in days, I feel a small bit of hope. Do you really think that Will might still be alive?"

"You know, I do. And do you know why? Because these people want that money. And you say you haven't paid it to them yet?"

"No. I'm supposed to tape it to our mail box tomorrow night."

"So, obviously they need to keep Will alive at least until they pick up the money, because if you refused or they discovered that you hadn't put the money there, they could threaten you by showing you his picture. And if they had already killed him it would be an idle threat."

"That is true," she said, now quieter and more thoughtful. "Mrs.——?"

"Essie…"

"Essie, everything you say makes perfect sense."

"And now I'm going to say one more thing that I hope you will realize also makes sense. And that is, you have to contact the police. I know these criminals told you not to, but think of it this way. It's unlikely that they are listening in on your phone calls. They would have no way of knowing if you contacted the police. I suggest you contact them immediately. This is definitely a police matter. These people are criminals and need to be arrested."

"I know that, Essie. I just don't want to lose Will in the process. I'm afraid."

"The police understand how to handle these things, Carolyn. You have to trust them."

"Maybe. I believe you. I'll think about it."

"And Carolyn, call me tomorrow and let me know what happens."

"I will, Essie. Thank you."

Chapter 19

Again, Essie couldn't sleep. She tossed and turned, worrying about Carolyn and wondering if she really would contact the police. Essie had had her encounters with the authorities in the past, and although she'd had her own doubts about them, she felt that in the long haul, it was best to leave actual criminal activity to the police. And this situation with Carolyn was definitely a criminal activity.

When she got up and had gotten dressed, she headed out to her living room and went straight to her window. She lifted the side of the blinds up and searched around for Red. Within a few seconds, the jaunty little bird landed on the nearby branch and faced directly into her living room.

"Well, there you are," she said to him. "Where did you go the other day? I thought maybe you had disappeared on me, and I've had too many people disappearing recently. I don't need you zipping off too."

The bird flitted from one end of the branch to the next, looked around, and then took off without a good-bye to Essie.

Soon, Joey arrived with her breakfast and with a message of gratitude from his family.

"Miss Essie," he said, coming over and giving her a warm hug——which wasn't easy with all that personal protective spacesuit gear he was wearing.. "This was all your doing, wasn't it?"

"I swear I don't know what you're talking about, Joey," she replied with a smile.

"This," he said, walking over to her laptop on her coffee table and typing in the address for the funding page they had set up for his family's restaurant. "You and your lady friends did this, didn't you?"

"Well, we had a lot of help from my grandson, Ned," she admitted.

"Look, Miss Essie. This site has raised over a thousand dollars to help my parents. I can't believe it. My parents don't even understand how it works, and I had to explain it to them. They're just overwhelmed with joy and gratitude, and they told me to tell you thank you."

"Well, Joey, Ned set up the site——at our prompting. It's because your parents are so beloved in this community that people want to help them out during this terrible time."

"It's just the nicest thing," he said. "No one has ever done anything like this for..." He rubbed the plastic mask covering his face as if he were rubbing away tears.

"Oh, Joey, it was our great pleasure," she said. "I only hope it helps your parents, and your family's restaurant can weather the pandemic okay and go on to serve our community for many years to come."

"Me too," he said, obviously at a loss for words. "I'd better get going."

"Okay," she said. "And that hug you gave me?"

"Yes?"

"Can you share it with your parents?"

"Of course, Miss Essie," he replied, putting his arms around her shoulders again and squeezing. "See you at lunch time." He left.

After Joey had departed, Essie felt a wonderful wave of happiness. She was glad that something she had worked on recently had come to such a meaningful fruition. Now, if only she could help Carolyn.

She vowed to give Carolyn some time before she went rushing in as was her typical bull-in-a-china shop tendency. She knew the woman would need to gather the courage to call the police and explain her situation. But she also knew that time was limited. She had to do something before tonight when Carolyn was expected to tape the ransom money to her mailbox. The police would need time to arrange a plan to catch the kidnappers——or rather——dog-nappers. Essie knew that Carolyn was an hour ahead of her as far as time zones went, so it was now after nine a.m. where she lived. She decided to wait until lunchtime, and if she hadn't heard from Carolyn by then, she would call her back and see what was going on. She knew that she was not going to wait all day and leave this all to chance.

She spent the morning watching news programs. How dreary. All they reported on was the pandemic. It was so depressing. Now she realized why she didn't watch much television anymore. Some reporters said things would get better soon, and others said things would get worse. *They don't know anything*, thought Essie.

She turned off her television and wheeled herself over to her laptop. It was still plugged in and still open to Joey's 'Save Me' page. She glanced down at the amount that had been donated so far, and it was closing in on two thousand dollars. Vicar's knickers! This was amazing. She sat on her sofa and spent some time reading the information on the site. She learned about the restaurant—how long it had been there, the menu, the owners and their background. *Joey is such a wonderful young man,* thought Essie. She could see why; his parents seemed like wonderful, hard-working people. *They certainly make good pizza,* she thought to herself.

She resolved to give Pru a call and see about setting up a credit card account for herself so she could order pizza whenever she wanted it. It was ridiculous to have to have her daughter order her food for delivery. She was an adult with money of her own; she could order a pizza when she wanted. Of course, she knew she'd have to wait to call Pru; today she needed to leave her phone line open in case Carolyn called with news about the dog-nappers.

The morning dragged on. By eleven, Essie was getting worried. Surely Carolyn had had time to contact the police in Bancroft Falls. It was noon there. Why hadn't she called back? Should Essie call her? Or was she being horribly impatient? She didn't want to antagonize the woman. On the other hand, she really needed to be sure that Carolyn called the police for her own protection. She could lose ten thousand dollars *and* her dog if she didn't. Essie tapped her foot. She rolled her walker around her apartment thinking she was getting some exercise. She checked on Red through her window, but he wasn't around. She surmised that her little bird friend only made personal visits in the very early morning hours.

Around noon, Joey returned with her lunch. Essie realized that time was flying by and she became even more worried.

"What's wrong, Miss Essie?" he asked.

"I'm waiting to hear from Carolyn," she said.

"Oh, the lady who popped in on your Zoom meeting?"

"Yes. She's supposed to call me. Joey, I'm afraid she's in real trouble. She said she'd call me back. She promised she'd call the police and let them help her. I thought she'd have called me by now."

"It's only noon, Miss Essie."

"It's one o'clock where Carolyn lives."

"Some people just don't get started until the afternoon."

"But Carolyn is worried sick about her dog."

"Her dog?"

"Yes—Will. Her dog is Will. That's who's been kidnapped. They took her dog and are holding him for a ten thousand dollar ransom."

"Oh, then she definitely needs to call the police."

"I know. That's what I told her, but she's afraid these dog-nappers will kill Will if she gets the police involved."

"Oh, Miss Essie, I'm sure she'll have much better results and remain safer——I might add——if the police are involved. She shouldn't be trying to deal with a bunch of kidnappers on her own——"

"Dog-nappers."

"Dog-nappers. Whatever. Either way. She should call the police."

"That's what I told her. She said she would, and she said she'd call me back when she did. Now the fact that she hasn't called me back makes me think she's changed her mind."

"Maybe. There could be——"

"She's supposed to leave the ransom money taped to her mailbox tonight."

"Oh my," said Joey, shaking his plastic-covered head. "That sounds really scary. That lady should not be doing that on her own."

"Yes," said Essie. "That's what I told her."

"I don't know what to tell you, Miss Essie. Are you thinking of calling the police yourself?"

"I am. I think I'll call her back first, and if she doesn't respond, I think I'll contact the Bancroft Falls police. There's a deadline. The dog-nappers gave her until tonight to put the ten thousand dollars on her mailbox. The police need to know about this before it gets dark."

"Agreed. I need to get going. I have a lot of trays to deliver yet. Are you going to be okay, Miss Essie? Should I call anyone to come up to see you?"

"No," she said. "I can phone if I need anything. I'll be Zooming with my friends and my grandson at three. I'll ask their opinion before I do anything final."

"That sounds like a good idea," he said, then he departed.

Chapter 20

Essie was miserable the next few hours. She kept looking at the clock. She wanted to present her predicament to the entire group at three. She felt that with all of their input, whatever she decided to do would surely be right. Also, she hoped that maybe by three Carolyn would have called her. But that possibility was looking less and less likely as the day went on.

She still had an unfinished crossword puzzle from her morning's puzzle sheet. She sat in her recliner after lunch and worked on it, thinking it would distract her. It didn't.

She checked again on Red. There was still no sign of the cardinal.

A little before three, Essie went to her bathroom to clean up. She was becoming aware of how she looked on the Zoom, and so she spent more time fiddling with her hair and powdering her nose extra hard. She realized she was being vain but saw no reason not to look her best, and now that she could actually see how she looked to others, she was more motivated to pay special attention to her appearance.

Shortly before three, as had become her habit, she headed to her sofa and turned on her computer. The screen popped open to Joey's Save Me page. Just the sight of it made Essie smile. She was so happy that at least one thing in her world was really going right. She clicked on her Zoom screen and checked out her camera and audio. At exactly three, just as she had in her previous meetings, she clicked the "launch" button, and the meeting opened up the entire screen, showing Essie in her little square up at the top as the host. Shortly afterwards Fay's image popped up and Fay waved to Essie. Essie returned her greeting. In another few moments, Opal and Marjorie arrived almost at the exact same time.

"Hello, Essie," said Opal.

"Hello, Essie," said Marjorie.

"Hello, Fay," said Opal.

"Hello, Fay," said Marjorie.

Essie returned their greetings, and Fay waved again. There was some pleasant chit chat as the ladies waited for Ned to arrive. After a good five minutes of chatting, Essie spoke up.

"Hmm," she said. "I wonder where Ned is. He told me he'd join us, just like he's been doing."

"Well," said Opal, "maybe something came up. I mean, he does have an actual job, Essie."

"I know that, Opal," replied Essie, "but he knows how important our meeting is today."

"I think we can handle things without him, Essie," suggested Marjorie. "We're all smart."

"Well, some of us are," stated Opal.

"Now, Opal," said Essie. "Let's not bicker among ourselves. I guess we can get started, and when Ned gets here, we'll just fill him in."

"Great," said Marjorie. "Do you have any news, Essie? I

mean about Carolyn?"

"I do," said Essie proudly. "I spoke with her yesterday."

This piece of information was met with gasps from all except Fay, who responded with hands waving above her head.

"Ned confirmed yesterday that the Carolyn we met on our Zoom meeting and the woman on the answering machine at the Carl Harper residence were the same person. So, knowing that, I called the Carl Harper number and left a message for Carolyn, explaining why I was calling and assuring her that I was absolutely no threat to her and telling her how we had all become worried about her since she had popped into our Zoom meeting the other day."

"Did she pick up the phone?" asked Opal.

"No, she didn't," said Essie. "I thought it was a lost cause, but last night right before I went to bed, she called me. At first, she was screaming at me like she was mad at me, but I tried very hard to calm her down. It was difficult, but I believe I convinced her that I wasn't a bad person and that I wasn't trying to harm this Will of hers."

"So, Essie," said Marjorie, "why is she so upset? What is she afraid of?"

"And who is Will?" asked Opal.

"It turns out that Will is her dog."

"Her dog?" declared Opal and Marjorie at the same time.

"Yes, apparently someone took him."

"You mean kidnapped him?" asked Marjorie.

"Well, dognapped him," said Essie. "Yes, and poor Carolyn is distraught. They left a ransom note taped to her front door. There was an internet link which supposedly was connected to a live feed of Will to prove to Carolyn that he was still alive. She doesn't have a computer, so that's why she walked to the senior center. She was trying to see her dog on the internet.

The criminals left her orders to get ten thousand dollars from the bank in hundred-dollar bills and put it in an envelope and tape it to her mail box this evening."

"You mean she hasn't given them any money yet?"

"No, the drop off is scheduled for tonight," said Essie. "And she plans to go through with it because she wants Will back."

"Then we have to stop her," said Opal.

"We need to contact the police," said Marjorie.

"Just wait a minute. I tried to talk her into doing just that. She was supposed to call me back and let me know once she'd contacted them, but she hasn't called yet."

"She probably chickened out," said Marjorie.

"That's what I'm afraid of," said Essie. "So what do I do now? I'm afraid once she tapes that envelope of money to her mailbox, she'll never see her dog again."

"Or her money," added Opal, as usual the practical one of the group.

"Where's Ned?" asked Marjorie.

"Yes, Essie," said Opal. "Isn't he supposed to be here for our meeting?"

"He said he'd be here," replied Essie. "Maybe he's just running late. This is just a…"

"Side gig," said Marjorie.

"Yes," said Essie. "He's already devoted so much of his time to helping us…"

"I know," said Opal, "but I wish I knew what he thought we should do."

"And I wish he'd be the one to do it," said Marjorie. "I mean, Essie, if someone's going to call the police, I think it should be a man. They'll pay more attention to a man."

"You're being ridiculous, Marjorie," replied Essie. "I've

talked to lots of policemen in my day, and they pay attention to me."

"Well, Essie," said Opal. "It's quite clear that this Carolyn is not going to join us, and she's obviously not going to call you back, for whatever reason."

"And I think it's also clear that Ned has flown the coop," said Marjorie.

"He has not flown the coop," replied Essie. "Fay," she said to the sweet face smiling in the left-hand corner of her screen, "what do you think we should do?" Fay bit her lip, obviously thinking, then she bent her head and appeared to be typing. When she looked up, they all clicked on the "Chat" button where Fay had typed in, "Essie, call police now. We can't wait for Ned."

"Well, that's that," said Essie, looking all around at her friends. They all looked back at her. She felt as if all the responsibility had fallen on her shoulders, and she was petrified.

Chapter 21

After the Zoom meeting had ended, Essie sat on her sofa and thought. She had never been so undecided in her life. She was so afraid that if she called the police, they would just laugh at her. After all, the thought of someone kidnapping a dog and asking for ten thousand dollars in ransom seemed incredibly unlikely. If only Ned were here to give her advice——or better yet, make the call himself.

Stop it, Essie, she thought. *You are not some damsel in distress. You do not need a man to solve all your problems and fight all your battles. You are perfectly capable of contacting the police in this little town and explaining the problem and getting them to do something before it's too late.*

"Take the bull by the horns," she said out loud. With those words, she shoved her walker back to her recliner and called the main desk for a long distance operator.

"Operator," said the voice.

"I want to call the Bancroft Falls, New York Police Department," she said to the woman.

"One moment," replied the operator. It was more than a moment, but eventually she was connected.

"Bancroft Falls P.D.," said a male voice. "How may I direct your call?"

"I'm not certain," replied Essie. "I need to talk to someone about a crime that has been committed, or is possibly about to be committed…"

"One moment," said the man. Essie prepared for another long wait.

"Detective Pelfrey," said a new voice rather quickly. "How may I help you?"

"Um, hello," said Essie. "My name is Essie Cobb. I don't live in Bancroft Falls, but recently I met a lady who does live there and she's in some trouble. I tried to talk her into calling you and getting help, but I'm afraid she hasn't done so."

"Yes, ma'am," said the detective. "Just a minute. Let me get your information down." He recorded Essie's name, phone number, and address, then asked her to continue.

"Several days ago, when my friends and I were having a Zoom meeting, this woman we didn't know popped up on our screen. She was scared and worried and looking for someone she called Will. We all assured her we didn't know Will or where he was. Then she just disappeared. We were able to track her down using my friend's excellent computer skills, so that is how we found out she lived in Bancroft Falls. Anyway, to make a long story short, I spoke with her yesterday, and it turns out Will is her dog, and he has been taken by someone who is demanding she give them ten thousand dollars in ransom tonight."

"Mrs. Cobb," said the detective, in a voice sounding grave. "You say this woman lives here in Bancroft Falls?"

"Yes, her name is Carolyn Harper." Essie gave the officer

Carolyn's phone number and address.

"These crooks have told Carolyn to leave an envelope with the ten thousand dollars in it taped to her mailbox tonight if she ever wants to see her dog again."

"Hmm," said the detective. "Tonight?"

"Yes. Can you go over to her house? Can you catch these hoodlums when they show up to take her money? And can you figure out a way to do it and save her dog too?"

"Mrs. Cobb, can you hold for a minute?"

"Yes, but please let's not take too much time. She's supposed to tape the money to the mailbox tonight."

"I understand, Mrs. Cobb." Essie heard a click and then piped in elevator music. She was extremely frustrated. *They probably just think I'm some crazy old woman with a bee in her bonnet,* she thought. She drummed her fingers to the music.

A few minutes later, the phone was answered by the same policeman she'd spoken to before. "Mrs. Cobb?"

"Yes, that's me," she said.

"I'm going to transfer you to our fraud unit. Detective Malloy. Hold on."

Essie held on. That is, she waited. In a few seconds, another man was speaking to her.

"Mrs. Cobb?"

"Yes, that's me."

"This is Detective Malloy with the fraud unit. Can you tell me about this conversation you had with this lady? You say she lives here in Bancroft Falls?"

"Yes, detective," said Essie. "Her name is Carolyn Harper, and she lives at 1203 Rose Street. I met her on a Zoom meeting a few days ago. I didn't really find out what her problem was then, only that she was terribly upset…"

"And why was that?"

"Her dog had been stolen," said Essie. "Well, at the time I thought it was her husband. She just said they had Will. I assumed Will was her husband. She was terribly upset during our meeting and then she just left. The last few days my friends and I have spent all our time trying to find her. I just found her last night. She told me someone had stolen her dog and told her to leave ten thousand dollars in hundred dollar bills in an envelope taped to her mailbox tonight."

"Tonight?"

"Yes, that's why it's important to do something now. She told me she would call the police there, but I'm guessing that....uh, that she didn't."

"No, she didn't. This is the first we've heard of this case."

"This case?"

"Yes, I mean of Carolyn Harper's case. We have numerous other instances of this particular group scamming other elderly ladies who own pets and demanding a ransom in ways similar to this one, asking them to tape money to an outside mailbox."

"You have?"

"Oh yes," he said. "This is a ruthless gang. We haven't been able to catch them for the very reason that you seem to be having trouble getting your friend Carolyn to come see us. The victims are all afraid that if they come to the police, they'll never see their pets again. And they're right. They don't ever see them again——or their money. But you calling us gives us a chance to catch them. Especially as the drop-off is tonight."

"Oh, I do hope so."

"Okay, Mrs. Cobb. I think we have the information we need. All I ask is that if you hear from Mrs. Harper any time tonight, please don't reveal that you've informed the Bancroft Falls Police Department of her dilemma. We're going to catch these crooks tonight if I have anything to say about it. Thank you again for the heads up."

"You're welcome, Detective Malloy. And, can you either call me when this is over——or have Carolyn call me, if she's willing? She's probably going to be pretty steamed at me for calling you."

"She shouldn't be. If her dog is still alive and has any chance of making it through this, you're the one she should thank for it."

"Oh, well, I just want her to be safe——and not lose her dog or her money."

"That's what we all want, Mrs. Cobb. That's what we all want."

Chapter 22

After Essie finished talking to the Bancroft Police, she hung up and practically collapsed in her recliner. *Thank goodness, I'm already seated,* she thought, *because if I wasn't, I'd fall down right here and now.*

Her phone rang.

"Mom," the voice said.

"Oh, hello, dear," she said, recognizing Pru's voice. "I could surely use some of that mint liqueur right now."

"Mom, Shanna's in the hospital."

"What?" she asked, sitting up abruptly. "What's wrong?"

"They don't know. Ned had to rush home from his convention. He's with her now. Claudia went over to stay with the baby."

"Is that safe? I thought she couldn't be with the baby because of the pandemic."

"Well, I think it's safer for the baby to be with his grandmother at home than be dragged to a hospital full of a lot of sick people. Besides, babies hardly ever get Covid. And besides that, Ned needs to be able to concentrate on Shanna."

"So, that's why he wasn't in our Zoom meeting," Essie mumbled. What happened to Shanna? What are her symptoms?"

"She just collapsed. Claudia said Shanna phoned her but was hardly able to speak, so Claudia rushed over to their house. By the time she got there, Shanna was old cold on the floor. Claudia called the paramedics and they took her to the hospital. Claudia stayed with the baby. That's what the paramedics recommended she do for everyone concerned. Claudia called Ned and he took the first plane back. I guess his boss is extremely apologetic for even making Ned travel while his wife was at home with a newborn. Now with her sick, Ned's boss is just falling all over himself to apologize. It's pretty obvious how much Ned is valued at that place."

"Well, that's good. At least now Shanna can get some care. And they can find out why she's so tired and despondent."

"I truly hope so. But I'm also worried about Claudia. I just hope she hasn't exposed herself to that horrible virus."

"From a newborn baby? I doubt it."

"You never know, Mom."

"Anyway, I'm glad to hear that Ned is there now. I was wondering why he never showed up to our Zoom meeting today."

"Oh, you had another one of those?"

"Yes, we've been meeting daily trying to figure out who this lady is who popped up on our screen during our first meeting. She was so worried and scared. We just wanted to find her and help her."

"And did you?"

"Believe it or not, I think we did. It's a long story, Pru. I'd kind of like to wait until I get a chance to tell Ned before I explain it all to everyone else."

"Of course, Mom. If I hear from Claudia, I'll tell her to have him call you."

"Oh no. This can wait. He should be with Shanna first."

"Yes, of course. But if he gets a chance…"

"Okay, but only if he has time and is not totally exhausted," she added.

"Exhausted," Essie repeated after she and her daughter had said goodbye. She slid down into her recliner and——just for a second——closed her eyes. She was awakened, it seemed, a few minutes later by the ringing phone. She glanced at her watch and saw that it was ten thirty at night. Essie had fallen asleep in her chair—and had been asleep for hours!

She had just a second to note that her telephone had become the focus of all of her social activity during this horrible pandemic. All joy. All sorrow. All suspense. It was all centered right here in her little telephone set. The good news came in through this device, and so did the bad news. She picked up the receiver.

"Hello."

"Mrs. Cobb?" asked a male voice. "This is Detective Malloy. Sorry to bother you so late…"

"Oh, Detective, that's fine," she replied. "How is Carolyn? Did you find her dog? Did you arrest the gang?"

"Yes to all your questions, Mrs. Cobb. I thought you might be anxious to hear the results of our raid. I'm sorry if I woke you."

"No, I was waiting for your call." Essie considered this only a small white lie. She was, after all, waiting——although she was doing it while napping.

"Anyway, Mrs. Harper is safe. We arrested a group of five young men. They've been running this ring from a van where they also keep the dogs that they steal locked in cages. We found Mrs. Harper's dog in a cage inside the van, safe and sound. He's been reunited with Mrs. Harper. I wish I could say the same for the seven or eight other dogs still in cages there. We'll try to find their owners, but I don't hold out much hope for them. Anyway, just as you explained to us, we had Mrs. Harper follow the gang's orders ostensibly. She went out and taped an envelope to her mailbox a little after dark. We had undercover agents patrolling the area. Shortly after she taped up the envelope and returned back inside, a young fellow came along and discreetly removed the envelope, opened it, counted the money, then signaled a van that was parked down the street which quickly met up with him, and he jumped inside. No sooner was he in the car than our agents pulled out into the street and blocked the van. All of our agents pulled their guns, and the gang of guys dropped to the ground. None of them had weapons. We quickly arrested them all and took them to our local jail for processing. We of course had to confiscate Mrs. Harper's money in the envelope, but it will be returned to her after the trial. We did let her keep her dog at home, even though technically we should have kept him, but he was such a scared little fellow, and when he saw your friend, Mrs. Harper, he just went crazy with joy."

"Oh I'm so glad," said Essie.

"I suppose she asked how you knew about the money and the dog stealing."

"Yes, she said to me, and I quote, 'I guess that crazy Essie lady called you, didn't she?'"

"Crazy? Hmmm," said Essie. "I've been called worse."

"Something tells me you have," he said with a smile. "Anyway, I'm happy to have you on my team anytime——crazy or not——Miss Essie. Thank you for your help, and please let me know if there's anything I can do to repay you."

"There's nothing I can think of," she said. Then suddenly, changing her mind, she added, "Do you like pizza?"

"Who doesn't?" he asked.

"We're trying to support a local pizza restaurant down here where I live. The pandemic has almost closed it for good. We have a 'Save Me' page on the internet. Just look up Joey Rizzoli. You'll find it."

"That I can do, Miss Essie," he replied. "I've contributed to a number of those fund me pages for lots of businesses that are struggling during this awful virus thing. I'll be happy to contribute to yours. And I'll get all the guys in the precinct here to contribute too. Joey Rizzoli. Got it."

They parted, laughing about their fondness for pizza. Essie didn't tell him that her fondness had only rather recently developed.

As was becoming a pattern, her phone rang again as soon as she hung up.

"Grandma," cried Ned. "I'm so sorry I missed the Zoom meeting today."

"Oh, Ned. Lordy Mordy," said Essie. "Don't apologize. You have a sick wife. You have a legitimate excuse."

"Even so, I feel bad for leaving you in the lurch right when things were sort of coming to a head…"

"Coming to a head is right," she said.

"Well, I'm at the hospital now. Shanna is sleeping and I slipped out of her room for a minute to check in with you. Please update me. What's going on?"

"Well, the Carolyn situation is much better. We know now what her problem was."

"And what was it?"

"A gang of thieves had kidnapped her dog."

"Her dog?" said Ned. "Oh, you mean Will is her dog?" *The light bulb went off in his head,* thought Essie.

"Yes. I spoke with her and she explained that these monsters dognapped him and demanded a hefty ransom to get him back…"

"Ransom? For her dog?"

"Yes, Ned. She's very attached to her dog. A lot of people are."

"I know, I know. Anyway…"

"Anyway she was supposed to leave an envelope full of money taped to her mailbox for them to pick up. And, supposedly, they'd return her dog if she did."

"I doubt they would," he said. "They'd probably kill him."

"Oh, no," said Essie. "That's why she was in our Zoom meeting. They gave her some sort of internet link or code that when she typed it in, she was supposed to see a live feed to Will——that's her dog."

"Yes, I remember."

"But she must have entered the digits wrong, because she got in our meeting instead. Then she was just so frustrated and mad, she left and went home. But anyway, she still planned to give them the money. I finally got a hold of her and tried to talk her out of it but she refused and so I told the police anyway. So I suppose she's furious with me, but I'm glad I did anyway, because evidently this dognapping scam has been going on in Bancroft Falls for quite some time. A lot of people have lost their dogs and their money and the police were fit to be tied. So, I finally called the police because I knew Carolyn wouldn't. I told them about her and that she was going to leave her money on her mailbox. So they set up a sting operation and captured the crooks. There were a bunch of the rascals. And Carolyn got Will back——he was in a cage inside the crooks' van——and she'll get her money back after the investigation and the trial but that may be a while."

"Wow, Grandma," said Ned, "that is some story. You are a heroine."

"No, I just did what was right," she said. "Oh, and the detective wanted to thank me so I told him to contribute to Joey's Save Me page."

"Grandma, you are a true wheeler-dealer." He paused. "I wish we could fix all problems so easily," he said in a somber voice.

"Oh, Ned, here I am rambling on about this adventure of mine, and you're there worried sick about Shanna…"

"The best part of all of this is that it's finally been brought to light. The doctors realize that what Shanna has been experiencing is more than just a little post-partum depression now. She's verging on suicidal."

"Oh, Ned, no——" Essie gasped. "Do you think she would hurt herself? Or the baby?"

"The baby——no. Herself? That I'm not so sure about. But they're going to start her on medication and therapy. I'm so lucky that Mom can stay at our house and watch the baby."

"Believe me, Claudia does not consider watching that baby any sort of hardship…"

"She does really seem to like babies…"

"Well, certain babies," said Essie, smiling at her favorite grandson. Then she yawned. "Oh dear, I'm so sorry. It's getting late, and I really haven't gotten much sleep in the last few days."

"I know how worried you've been about Carolyn," he said. "Maybe now that you know she and her little dog are safe, you can relax and get a good night's sleep."

"Maybe so," she said.

"Well, I'm going to sign off, Grandma," he said. "Sleep tight. Hugs and kisses."

She blew him back a kiss of her own and put the telephone back in its spot.

Then, before she could fall back to sleep in her recliner, she heaved herself out of her chair, grabbed her walker, and headed off to bed.

Chapter 23

"Miss Essie. Miss Essie!" Someone was shoving her over a mountain top. Or at least it felt like someone was heaving her around. What was going on? "Miss Essie, I hate to wake you, but it's after eight in the morning. I have your breakfast. I just want to be sure you're okay."

"What?" she mumbled, turning over in her bed and shoving away the hand that was jostling her. "Go away."

"Miss Essie," said Joey, bending over her in his space helmet. Essie opened her eyes and screamed.

"Oh, Joey," she said. "It's you. Where am I?"

"You're still in bed. You must not have heard your alarm. It's after eight. I have your breakfast in the kitchen for you."

"Oh dear. I finally got some sleep last night," she said, yawning.

"Oh, Miss Essie, I'm so sorry I woke you up. I was just worried about you."

"It's okay, Joey. Can you just leave the tray? I'll get ready and get out there as soon as I can."

"No rush, Miss Essie," he said. "Here, I have my thermometer. Let me get a quick check, and then you can go back to sleep if you like." She opened her mouth and the obligatory test was accomplished.

"Fine, as usual," he stated. "Now, I'm out of here. Sweet dreams."

The young man was gone in an instant, and Essie remained in bed. It felt rather luxurious being so slovenly. She just lay there and thought about everything that had happened yesterday. *Oh my, what a wild ride.*

"Well, enough of that," she said out loud, now totally bored with being a lady of leisure. She kicked her legs over the edge of the bed, grabbed her walker, and proceeded to transfer from her nighttime sweats to her daytime sweats. She ambled with her walker to the kitchen and plopped her breakfast tray onto the seat, then moved over to her recliner, where she sat down and started her breakfast of some sort of flake cereal with apple slices in a bowl. She turned on her television and caught up on the news, which was primarily pandemic, pandemic, pandemic.

"How depressing," she said aloud. "I need to find something positive."

She stood up and rolled her walker over to her window, hoping that it wasn't too late for Red to be on his branch. When she looked between the slats of her blinds, she didn't see him. *Hmm*, she thought. *Where can he be?* She pulled up the blinds by the cord, allowing a blast of sunlight to invade her living room. She had to put her hand in front of her glasses, it was so bright. As soon as her eyes adjusted, she moved back to the window and stood quietly by its edge. She noticed some movement in the depths of the big evergreen. She waited. Shortly, she saw him. Red. But, oh my, he wasn't alone. He popped out onto the branch and was followed by his exact double——except for coloring. This second bird was brown all over with some small splotches of red here and there.

"You have a girlfriend, Red," said Essie softly, although she knew it was unlikely the bird could hear her through the glass. "Now that's a good way to handle boredom, little fellow. A lady for you. I think I'll call her 'Lady.' Red and Lady. I like it." Essie watched the two birds interact and jump around on the branch for a while, then she slowly lowered the blinds with the side cord and gave them their "privacy." It was a joyous break from all the excitement of the previous days' events.

Then she thought about everything that had happened yesterday with Carolyn, and the police and that horrible gang that was stealing pets from elderly ladies in Bancroft Falls. She felt so relieved that Carolyn had been reunited with her little dog Will. She assumed that Carolyn wouldn't return her calls because she was probably mad at her for going behind her back and calling the police. But it didn't matter. Essie was glad she'd gone behind her back because now Carolyn was safe, her dog was safe the police had caught the gang, and Carolyn would eventually get her money back. So be it if Carolyn hated Essie. It was worth it. Essie reasoned that sometimes you have to make difficult choices, and this had definitely been a difficult choice.

"I know," she said suddenly. "I'll check on Joey's funding site." She hobbled over to her laptop. She had left it plugged in from yesterday. She scolded herself but then realized that she routinely left lots of things plugged in——like her alarm clock——and she was checking the funding site a lot. It gave her a great deal of pleasure to see how much money people were donating to help out Joey's family. And again, as she looked down at the counter in the lower part of the site, she couldn't believe it when she saw that donors had given more than six thousand dollars to help the restaurant. This was so amazing to Essie——that strangers who didn't even know the Rizzoli family or who maybe had never even been to their restaurant were donating money to help keep it open. She also loved seeing the photos of Joey and her friends on the site. It brought back wonderful memories of when Ned had taken those photos and first set up the site.

"Hmm," she said, looking at the restaurant's menu. There were so many interesting dishes that the Rizzolis made. Not just pizza. "Yum," said Essie, as she scrolled through the online menu. "That looks a lot more appetizing than what they bring up from the dining room here."

She sat there and thought. She realized that lots of people must be ordering food——and other things——online because of the pandemic. She decided to experiment. Putting the little computer on her lap, she put her finger on the little touch pad. She moved it around and clicked some things. Ned had explained all of this when he'd helped her set it up but she hadn't paid much attention. All she had really cared about were her Zoom meeting. Of course, she knew there was much more to the internet.

Some clicking and pushing around of her mouse and she soon found herself on the internet. A list of various sites she could visit popped up, and Essie clicked on some news sites. "Ooo, ick," she cried. "I get enough of this from television." She clicked around and discovered sites where she could learn things, sites where she could interact with people, and most commonly——sites where she could buy things. As Essie didn't need anything——or even really want anything—she didn't think much of that. But then, she thought about the pizza that she'd eaten from Rizzoli's and how much better it was than the pizza she was used to, and she began to wonder about things she might buy from the internet. She spent a good portion of the morning investigating her computer and various online sites. By lunchtime, she thought she was getting kind of good at exploring the internet.

When Joey arrived with her lunch, he found her typing away at her computer.

"Miss Essie, I didn't expect to see you on your computer. Do you have another group you are Zooming with?" he asked.

"No, Joey," she said. "I've discovered the internet. It's much bigger than Zoom."

"That it is, Miss Essie."

"You can buy things, not just order pizza from your restaurant," she noted.

"Oh, Miss Essie, if I wanted to, I could easily spend my entire paycheck——back when I had a paycheck——on the internet. Luckily, now I just turn it over to my folks. That sort of gets rid of temptation."

"Just how do you buy things, Joey?"

"Miss Essie," he said, "be careful. It's so easy to buy things and so easy to lose track of how much you're spending."

"So, how do you do it?"

"You usually just put in your credit card number, or if you have a Venmo or PayPal account, you use that…"

"That's my problem," Essie said. "I don't have a credit card."

"That's probably a good thing, Miss Essie," Joey said, bringing her lunch over to the sofa and setting it beside the computer. "Miss Essie, a lot of people spend a lot of money on the internet and get into major debt before they even realize it."

"Not me, Joey; I'm very frugal."

"The internet is very enticing," he replied. "They make it so easy to buy things. You just click your mouse."

"Well, it's all moot. I don't have a credit card. *Yet.* I'm thinking I'll ask my daughter to get me one so I can buy things online."

"Well, be careful." He gave her a smile and headed out. Essie nibbled at her lunch as she played with the computer. She was hoping that she'd hear from Carolyn but she was afraid the woman was mad at her because she'd taken it upon herself to inform the police about Carolyn's situation. It didn't matter because Essie knew she had done the right thing. She could discuss all of this with her friends at their regular three o'clock Zoom meeting.

She smiled when she thought about belonging to a group that had a regular meeting online. She may not be buying things and scooting all over the internet like some of the young people today, but she was an old lady who now did Zoom chats with her friends every day. She was proud of that.

The phone rang. Essie set down her fork and hustled over to her recliner so she could answer her phone. She so hoped it was Carolyn.

"Hi, Mom," said Prudence.

"Oh, hello, dear," responded Essie.

"You sound sad," said her daughter. "Or are you not happy to speak to me?"

"No, dear, I just thought you might be someone else."

"Not one of those old men at Happy Haven?" said Pru, sounding decidedly worried.

"No, no. Nothing like that. I was hoping you might be Carolyn Harper, the lady who we've been helping."

"I thought you were still trying to locate her," said Pru.

"Oh, I found her," said Essie, "but I'm not so certain she's thrilled at having been found. I'm afraid she might be a bit upset with me and what I've done…"

"What did you do, Mom?" said her daughter in a very accusatory fashion.

"Nothing bad," said Essie. "In fact, something very good."

"What, Mom?"

"Well, I was hoping to talk with Carolyn about that very thing. I thought you were her."

"Sorry. I'll go and you can wait for her call."

"No, wait a minute, Pru. I'd like a credit card."

"What? What brought this on?"

"I just realized as I sit here with the little computer that Ned got for me that the internet is a very amazing place and that there are lots of things you can buy there, but you need a credit card."

"Mom, I told you. If you need anything, I'll get it for you and bring it to you. That's the easiest way. Why on earth would you want to get all mixed up with a credit card? Then you have to keep track of that bill and remember to pay it. It's just a huge pain."

"Well, I want one," said Essie, huffing. She knew she sounded like a defiant toddler.

"Why don't we talk about it?"

"We are talking about it, and I want one," said Essie.

"Oh, Mom," declared Pru. "You have everything you could ever need right there. If you actually need something else, it's just as easy for me to bring it to you. Let me worry about your expenses. You having a credit card means one more thing I'd have to keep track of."

"No, you wouldn't," said Essie. "I can keep track of it myself. I'm an adult, and if once in a while I'd like to purchase something for myself without having to check it out with you for approval..."

"You don't need approval," said Pru.

"It's the same thing," said Essie. "Having to ask you is just like saying I need approval. Sometimes I just want to buy something and I don't want anyone else to know about it."

"Like what, Mom? Is this some sort of sex thing?"

"No, dear. Of course not," said Essie. "It's more like some sort of pizza thing."

"Oh," said her daughter. "So you've developed a taste for delivery pizza."

"Not just any delivery pizza——Rizzoli's delivery pizza. And I want to be able to order it by myself for myself when I want it. I'm an adult, and I should be able to do that."

"I guess so," said Pru with a sigh. "Let me see what I can do. I have to go to the bank this afternoon. I'll see about getting you a low interest card."

"Thank you, dear," said Essie. "That would be wonderful."

Chapter 24

It was almost time for their three o'clock Zoom meeting. Essie had hoped she would have heard from Carolyn before this. She really wanted to have something to report that would be good news to tell her friends. But it looked as if that was not to be. *Oh, Carolyn*, she thought. *I'm so sorry for betraying you. But I had to do what I did.*

She'd been to the bathroom for her touch up. She'd changed into a new shirt. She now was sitting in front of her laptop smiling into her Zoom screen. She could see herself in the little box, and she thought she looked better than she ever had. Her eyes were sparkling in the lenses of her glasses——that extra few hours of sleep had obviously done her a lot of good. Her head of gentle curls glistened. Her smile was——well——her regular Essie smile.

As the hand on her wristwatch hit three o'clock, Essie clicked the "launch" button for her Zoom meeting. The screen opened. Almost immediately, her three friends were there——Fay, Opal, and Marjorie.

"Hello, Essie," said Marjorie. "You look well."

"Hello, Marjorie."

"Hi, Fay."

Fay waved.

"Opal, how are you?"

"I'm well, Essie," said her prim friend. "You look a little smug, actually."

"Well, ladies," said Essie. "I do have some wonderful news to report."

All three women looked excited. Fay clapped her hands.

"Yes, Carolyn has been reunited with her dog." All three ladies responded excitedly in their little squares. Fay jumped up and down a bit in her wheel-chair. Opal and Marjorie cheered.

"And also, the police informed me that the people responsible for taking Will——her dog——were running this sort of ring where they were scamming people like Carolyn. The police there in Bancroft Falls had been trying to crack this gang for a long time. They were so grateful to hear from us so that they could capture these hoodlums before they could hurt Carolyn or steal her money or set up anyone else with this despicable scheme."

"Oh, Essie," said Opal. "That is truly a miracle. You contacted them just in time then."

"Well, yes," said Essie. "When I spoke with Carolyn…"

"She called you back?" asked Marjorie.

"No, so I decided to call the police myself because I knew that last night was the scheduled time for Carolyn to drop off the money, and I knew that once the bad guys had her money it would be too late to do anything. So I called the police there in Bancroft Falls, and as it turned out, they had been searching for this group for some time and were thrilled to get a tip. They set up a sting operation and when the gang went to pick up the money that Carolyn had left at the drop off point——which was the side of her mailbox——the police surrounded their van and arrested them all on the spot."

"That's amazing," said Marjorie. "You're a hero, Essie."

"No, I just got the right information to the people that needed it."

At that moment, another screen opened. Carolyn Harper, wearing a mask, appeared in a box. Her eyes were smiling, and she was holding a fluffy little dog.

"Hello," she said. "Which one of you is Essie?"

"That's me," said Essie. "And you're Carolyn?"

"That's me. And this is Will," she said with a gentle laugh. "He says hello and thank you." She whispered in the dog's ear, and he looked straight into the camera and barked twice. At that moment, three other people, all wearing masks appeared behind Carolyn.

"Oh, and these are all the people here at the Bancroft Falls Senior Citizens' Center who helped you find me——and Will," she said, motioning with her hand at the trio. "This is Phil, Gloria, and Phoebe." Each person nodded in turn and waved for the camera. "I can't thank them all enough for the part they played in helping me reunite with Will."

All four ladies from Happy Haven smiled and waved back. Once the greetings were made, the three workers took their leave, and Carolyn and Will were left alone in their screen box.

"I was afraid, Carolyn," said Essie, "that you were mad at me for going behind your back and contacting the police."

"Well, Essie," responded the gentle-looking face with a ring of blond curls surrounding it, "I guess I can take this off now," she said as she removed her mask. "I was mad, but then afterwards I realized that if you hadn't done what you did, I wouldn't have Will back now." She kissed the little dog on the top of his head and he nuzzled up against her cheek. She stifled a sob. It was very obvious that the two loved each other and were grateful to be reunited.

"I'm so happy," said Essie.

"And, Essie, since *you* did something without my approval, I guess you won't be able to complain if *I* do something without your approval," said Carolyn, with a twinkle in her eye.

"What's that?" said Essie.

"Oh, this," said Carolyn. She nodded her head to the left and suddenly another screen box popped open in which the image of a man appeared, below which showed the name "Detective Malloy."

"Hello, Detective," said Carolyn. "As you can see, they're all here. They meet at this location or this Internet address every day at three o'clock."

"So you said," replied Malloy, a nice-looking middle-aged man with a greyish crewcut and a mustache. "Happy to see you, Mrs. Harper and I see little Will seems to have recovered from his ordeal. I'm going to take this mask off for a while as no one is in my office at the moment. Anyway, good to see you both doing better."

"Yes, Detective, he's doing fine, now that he's home. Thanks to you and your department."

"But," said Malloy, "mostly thanks to you, Miss Essie." He looked into his camera, directly at Essie.

Essie couldn't help but blush, but apparently, blushing didn't convey very well over the internet.

"With you and your friends doing all this investigating and then——most importantly——contacting us before that gang could take Mrs. Harper's money, we were able to save little Will, recover Mrs. Harper's money, and put the whole gang away. Miss Essie, if you had waited any longer, we would not be seeing this reunion today. You all should know that this was a fairly long-standing and clever group. They counted on several things: an elderly single woman with a dog——a woman who they assumed would do anything, and pay anything to get their pet returned. They also counted on elderly people not being very computer savvy, that's why they gave them the Zoom link which connected to a feed of their pet in a cage. They assumed, and in many instances, rightly so, that elderly victims wouldn't have computers or wouldn't know how to connect to the Zoom link. Obviously, Mrs. Harper didn't have a computer, but she did go immediately to where she knew she could find one..."

"The Bancroft Falls Senior Citizens' Service Center," said everyone.

"But unfortunately, she was so nervous that she typed in the link to see her dog incorrectly on the center's computer and landed in the Zoom meeting with the four of you ladies instead. Very strange, but I guess it happens," he said.

"I'm just happy it all turned out so well," said Essie. "We all are. All four of us here were concerned and we all worked hard to try to figure it out from the minute Carolyn popped onto our screen to last night when I decided——against my better judgment——to contact your police department."

"Well, whether it was against your better judgment or not," continued Malloy, "we want to do something to honor your efforts. This arrest is a huge and meaningful one in our community and the entire area. Therefore, I have this proclamation." As he said these words, he held up a framed document adorned with a ribbon and gold seal. "It's from the mayor of Bancroft Falls, and it declares that Essie Cobb and her three companions are true heroes. You four will each receive one of these framed certificates signed by our mayor with your name engraved on it. Mrs. Harper, I will contact you later about seeing to it that these get to our ladies…"

"Detective," said Carolyn, "I will be happy to take care of seeing that the certificates get to the right ladies."

"Wonderful," he said, "then I guess I will leave you all to celebrate, as I have an office full of detectives who expect some sort of direction." He chuckled and gave them a short salute, and his box clicked off the screen.

"Wow," said Marjorie, "Essie, you're a hero."

"We all are," said Essie.

"Yes," said Carolyn, "certified by our mayor. I'm so happy about all of this. And so grateful to have my Will back. I'll never be able to thank you all. I feel now as if we are all friends."

"Well, Carolyn," said Essie, "with Zoom, it's easy to be friends because it's so easy for people to communicate even if they live far apart."

"So true," said Carolyn. Will barked in agreement, and they all laughed.

At that moment, a new box popped open. In it were Ned and Shanna. Shanna was wearing a hospital gown and she was in a hospital bed, but Ned was sitting beside her.

"Hey, Grandma," said Ned. "Just wanted to pop in on you ladies and say hi. Sorry I missed you the other day, ladies. Grandma, can explain. This is my wife, Shanna. She wasn't feeling well, but she's doing much better now." Shanna raised a hand attached to an IV and waved.

"Hi, Miss Essie," she said weakly.

"Hello, dear," said Essie. "We're so sorry to hear that you're not well, but I just bet that you will do much better now that Ned is back home."

"I will, I'm sure," replied Shanna softly, looking up at her husband sweetly.

"And who's caring for that sweet little baby?" asked Essie. But the answer was quickly forthcoming as a new box popped open and a lady holding a baby appeared.

"I heard something about a Zoom meeting," said Claudia, "and as I'm sitting here in a house full of computers, I found one attached to Zoom that I logged onto. I thought this sweet little fellow and I might drop in and say 'hi' to his mommy and daddy——and to his great-grandmother!"

Ned and Shanna waved and smiled at Claudia and their son.

"Oh, how sweet," said Marjorie.

"I hate to make you have to stay there and watch him, Claudia," said Shanna to her mother-in-law.

"Oh, Shanna," said Essie. "If you think you are *making* my daughter babysit that infant, then you don't know my daughter. There's nowhere she'd rather be. Nobody loves taking care of babies more than Claudia. She's probably hoping the two of you stay in that hospital a lot longer. She'll spoil that little guy rotten by the time you two get home."

"That's true, honey," said Ned to his wife. "I know my mom. She's probably in heaven to have our baby all to herself right now."

"You know it," said Claudia as she tweaked the baby's nose. The baby giggled and cooed. Everyone oooed.

Another screen popped open.

"Hi, Mom," said Prudence.

"Prudence, I didn't know you Zoomed too," said Essie.

"I felt as if I was missing out," replied Essie's oldest daughter. I made my husband set up the computer so I could join you. Claudia, is that you?"

"It's me, big sis," said Claudia, holding up the baby. "Look what I've got."

"Who is that?" asked Prudence.

"This is Ned and Shanna's newborn. This is baby Henry."

"Well, I'll be. Look at you. You're a grandma——and I'm a great-aunt."."

"I am and I love it," said Claudia.

"It suits you," said Prudence. "Seems like we should celebrate."

"You said it," said Essie. "And we have a lot to celebrate."

"Yes, most of you missed the big news," said Opal. "Essie received a commendation from the police department of Bancroft Falls, New York, for her assistance in foiling a gang of thieves. The lady in the box in the top row is Carolyn Harper. Essie saved her dog and her life savings."

"Wow, Mom," said Prudence. "I had no idea."

"Mom," said Claudia, "why do you keep these things to yourself?"

"It wasn't all me," said Essie, modestly. "All four of us—— me and Opal and Marjorie and Fay. We all received commendations from the mayor."

"We're proud of you all," said Ned.

"Well, Mom," said Prudence, "as you requested, I got you that credit card you wanted. I can bring it over now if you like so you can use it."

"Oh, yes, Pru," said Essie. "And I know just what I want to do."

As Pru waved good-bye and her box disappeared, another box opened; this one showed three people.

"Miss Essie," said Joey, now not wearing any protective gear. He was sitting between an older couple. "These are my parents. Mom, Dad, this is Miss Essie. The 'Save Me' site was her idea."

"Miss Essie," said the man sitting next to Joey, "how can we ever thank you?"

"This is the nicest thing anyone has ever done for us," added his wife.

"You see, Miss Essie," said Joey, "you have a fan club here."

"Miss Essie has a fan club in many places," said Ned. "Hey, when Aunt Pru gets there with your credit card, Grandma, may I suggest what your first purchase might be?"

"If you're thinking that I order pizza from Rizzoli's for everyone, that was my idea."

"I'll order one for Miss Carolyn from Nero's," said Ned. "I already know their number."

"Oh, look, Mom and Dad," said Joey, from his square, "our 'Save Me' page has just gone over ten thousand dollars."

"Wow!" said Ned. "It's really a coincidence that we just raised ten thousand dollars for Joey's family and at the same time saved Carolyn ten thousand dollars from that gang of dog-nappers. It must be a sign."

"Right," said Opal, "a sign that Essie Cobb can work miracles."

A cry of delight arose from the entire group of boxes on the screen. And as the conversation continued and the disparate group of individuals got to know each other better, they were soon interrupted by the sound of door bells ringing. People hurriedly left their screens and quickly returned holding Rizzoli pizzas (or in one case, a Nero's pizza).

Essie Cobb looked around the screen and smiled. She realized that she had made a whole bunch of new friends—in a very new and unusual way. And she had just one thing to say: "Take that, pandemic!"

Epilogue

The pandemic wore on, but Essie and her friends at Happy Haven didn't allow it to dampen their spirits. Now that they'd found Zoom, they worked together to bring the virtual togetherness to other residents. Ned was helpful in getting a grant for Happy Haven that provided laptops for all residents and Essie taught everyone at the facility how to Zoom——residents and staff alike!

They established virtual book clubs with Essie leading the mystery club, Marjorie the romance club, and Opal, the business literacy club. There was a virtual quilting club, a sit-and-knit club, a recipe exchange, and several game playing groups. There was even a "Birds outside Your Window" group led by Essie so that residents could truly appreciate their feathered friends living just inches away on the other side of their windows. Essie loved sharing her tales of Red and Lady——and their new nest of chicks that were born in the spring.

One other item of note, Essie continued to hear from Carolyn;

they spoke frequently via Zoom. Carolyn informed her that the Bancroft Falls Senior Citizens' Support Center had been instrumental in helping the——primarily elderly——victims of the dog-napping gang recover much or all of their savings. Also, the center was responsible for not only reuniting many owners with their pets, but in cases where pets had been lost due to the dog-nappers' behavior, finding new pet "babies" to replace the owner's original beloved creature.

Essie considered all of these developments good ones and she was grateful to Zoom for making them all possible.

About the Author

 Patricia Rockwell is the author of two mystery series. Her Pamela Barnes acoustic mysteries include *Sounds of Murder*, *FM for Murder*, *Voice Mail Murder*, *Stump Speech Murder*, and *Murder in the Round*. Her Essie Cobb senior sleuth mysteries include—in addition to this book *Zoomed—Bingoed*, *Papoosed*, *Valentined*, *Ghosted*, and *Firecrackered*.

Patricia is the founder and publisher of Cozy Cat Press, which specializes in producing cozy (or gentle) mysteries.

Dr. Rockwell is retired from college teaching. Her doctorate in Communication is from the University of Arizona. She was an Associate Professor at the University of Louisiana at Lafayette. She is presently living in Illinois with her husband, also a retired educator.

Made in the USA
Columbia, SC
01 April 2021